Pure Wicked

Also from Shayla Black/Shelley Bradley

EROTIC ROMANCE

The Wicked Lovers
Wicked Ties
Decadent
Delicious
Surrender To Me
Belong To Me
"Wicked to Love" (novella)
Mine To Hold
"Wicked All The Way" (novella)
Ours To Love
Wicked and Dangerous
"Forever Wicked" (novella)
Theirs To Cherish
Wicked All Night
His to Take
Coming Soon:
Pure Wicked (e-novella)
Wicked for You (October 6, 2015)

Sexy Capers
Bound And Determined
Strip Search
"Arresting Desire" – Hot In Handcuffs Anthology

The Perfect Gentlemen (by Shayla Black and Lexi Blake)
Scandal Never Sleeps
Seduction in Session (January 5, 2106)
Big Easy Temptation (May 3, 2016)

Masters Of Ménage (by Shayla Black and Lexi Blake)
Their Virgin Captive
Their Virgin's Secret
Their Virgin Concubine
Their Virgin Princess
Their Virgin Hostage
Their Virgin Secretary
Their Virgin Mistress
Their Virgin Bride (spring/summer 2016)

Doms Of Her Life (by Shayla Black, Jenna Jacob, and Isabella LaPearl)
One Dom To Love
The Young And The Submissive
The Bold and The Dominant
The Edge of Dominance (winter/spring 2016)

Stand Alone Titles
Naughty Little Secret (as Shelley Bradley)
Watch Me (as Shelley Bradley)
Dangerous Boys And Their Toy
"Her Fantasy Men" – Four Play Anthology

PARANORMAL ROMANCE

The Doomsday Brethren
Tempt Me With Darkness
"Fated" (e-novella)
Seduce Me In Shadow
Possess Me At Midnight
"Mated" – Haunted By Your Touch Anthology
Entice Me At Twilight
Embrace Me At Dawn

HISTORICAL ROMANCE (as Shelley Bradley)

The Lady And The Dragon
One Wicked Night
Strictly Seduction
Strictly Forbidden

Brothers in Arms
His Lady Bride, Brothers in Arms (Book 1)
His Stolen Bride, Brothers in Arms (Book 2)
His Rebel Bride, Brothers in Arms (Book 3)

CONTEMPORARY ROMANCE (as Shelley Bradley)
A Perfect Match

Pure Wicked

A Wicked Lovers Novella

By Shayla Black

1001 Dark Nights

EVIL EYE
CONCEPTS

Pure Wicked
A Wicked Lovers Novella
Copyright 2015 Shelley Bradley LLC
ISBN: 978-1-940887-61-6

Foreword: Copyright 2014 M. J. Rose

Published by Evil Eye Concepts, Incorporated

Sign up for the 1001 Dark Nights Newsletter
and be entered to win a Tiffany Key necklace.

There's a contest every month!

Go to www.1001DarkNights.com to subscribe.

As a bonus, all subscribers will receive a free
1001 Dark Nights story
The First Night
by Lexi Blake & M.J. Rose

One Thousand and One Dark Nights

Once upon a time, in the future...

*I was a student fascinated with stories and learning.
I studied philosophy, poetry, history, the occult, and
the art and science of love and magic. I had a vast
library at my father's home and collected thousands
of volumes of fantastic tales.*

*I learned all about ancient races and bygone
times. About myths and legends and dreams of all
people through the millennium. And the more I read
the stronger my imagination grew until I discovered
that I was able to travel into the stories... to actually
become part of them.*

*I wish I could say that I listened to my teacher
and respected my gift, as I ought to have. If I had, I
would not be telling you this tale now.
But I was foolhardy and confused, showing off
with bravery.*

*One afternoon, curious about the myth of the
Arabian Nights, I traveled back to ancient Persia to
see for myself if it was true that every day Shahryar
(Persian: شهريار, "king") married a new virgin, and then
sent yesterday's wife to be beheaded. It was written
and I had read, that by the time he met Scheherazade,
the vizier's daughter, he'd killed one thousand
women.*

*Something went wrong with my efforts. I arrived
in the midst of the story and somehow exchanged
places with Scheherazade – a phenomena that had
never occurred before and that still to this day, I
cannot explain.*

Now I am trapped in that ancient past. I have taken on Scheherazade's life and the only way I can protect myself and stay alive is to do what she did to protect herself and stay alive.

Every night the King calls for me and listens as I spin tales. And when the evening ends and dawn breaks, I stop at a point that leaves him breathless and yearning for more. And so the King spares my life for one more day, so that he might hear the rest of my dark tale.

As soon as I finish a story... I begin a new one... like the one that you, dear reader, have before you now.

Chapter One

May - Austin, Texas

Wasn't regret a bitch? In fact, Jesse McCall couldn't remember another time in his life when it had come off its leash and humped his leg so thoroughly.

As he emerged from the modern, mostly glass hotel, flashbulbs burst in his face, blinding him. He paused as reporters shouted questions his way. Beside him, his shark of a publicist, Candia, barked "no comment" in a nonstop loop as she led him to the waiting limo at the end of the crowded walk.

Jesse glanced at the big blue sky. Late afternoon blistered. Had it already been more than twelve hours since everything had gone so wrong? Why hadn't he asked more questions or hung around longer? Something that might have prevented this fucking tragedy...

Raking a hand through his hair, he squinted as he dragged his gaze over the surrounding skyscrapers. He was in some downtown area. Austin. Yeah. Half the time he woke up and didn't know what day it was, what city he'd preformed in, or who the hell he was lying next to. The life of a musician was frenetic and nomadic. Jesse had sold out one stadium tour after another since age sixteen. Twelve years later, he didn't know any other way to live.

He reached into his pocket and tossed on a pair of Armani shades, thanking god he wasn't hung over. A year of sobriety had ensured that, but still Candia strode beside him on her usual platforms, tense and waiting to flay him alive with her tongue the second they were alone.

When the limo driver opened the door of the sleek black stretch, Jesse climbed in behind his publicist as she settled into the leather seat and smoothed back the professional twist of her dark hair. Their chauffeur enclosed them together in the back of the car, and Jesse counted down to Candia's imminent explosion.

"Damn it, we're still on tour. The album just dropped last week." She tossed her gray Prada briefcase onto the floorboard and shot him a frustrated stare. "The bad-boy image has always worked for you because you're young and hot. But the public will view this as over the line. You want to give me the whole story now?"

As if she hadn't heard every word he'd told the pair of detectives over the last three hours. Did she honestly think he'd held back? The interview had finally ended when they'd realized he knew nothing and hadn't been in any way involved. Then the paunch-bellied one with the scowl had asked him to sign an autograph for his teenage daughter. With a few strokes of his pen, Jesse had been out the door.

"It's already public knowledge?" He'd hoped she could keep a lid on this until he could figure out what to do, how to process, what to say.

"TMZ and Perez Hilton are all over this shit. You even made CNN."

So that was a yes. He sighed. "I swear, I don't know anything else. After the show last night, Ryan caught me as I was leaving my suite. He said he'd met a girl and asked to borrow my room since he couldn't find the key to his own. He was in too much of a hurry to get under her miniskirt to fetch another one from the front desk."

Of course Ryan had invited him to join in, too. Girls and drugs, just like the good ol' days. Jesse had declined and begged Ryan to come with him. No dice.

"Then you went out for a ride?" Candia asked.

He nodded. "Cruising around on my motorcycle helps clear my head after a show."

And kept him away from the partying that had nearly ruined him over ten years of his career.

"Did you get a good look at her before you left?"

"You mean, did I know she was only sixteen? No. I barely glanced at her but I would have pegged her at well over twenty-one." Definitely not a sophomore in high school.

"If you'd made him go to the lobby, maybe someone would have stopped him... Maybe he would have used the head up north." She pressed her thumb between her eyebrows, obviously fighting off a headache. "Maybe… But it's done."

He wanted to be pissed that Candia had put this off on him, but she hadn't voiced anything he hadn't already thought. "At the time, I figured if Ryan was screwing some cute blonde, maybe he wasn't getting high."

Jesse scoffed at the terrible irony of that.

"Oh, he absolutely was. And he got her high, too."

Yes, his bandmate and old buddy had overdosed the girl—in Jesse's room. So naturally, everyone assumed he'd been involved.

"The press is having a field day." At barely four thirty in the afternoon, Candia already sounded damn tired.

Jesse could guess who they'd cast in the role of scapegoat, even though he hadn't been in the building when Ryan had pumped his jailbait hookup full of heroin and taken her to bed. Then, once his backup vocalist had realized the girl was unresponsive, he hadn't called 911 for medical help so she might have lived. No. He'd apparently panicked and shot himself in the head, doubling the tragedy.

Besides being a PR nightmare, Jesse had lost a friend he'd been trying to save. And the staggered, grief-stricken looks on the faces of that girl's parents when they realized their daughter was gone would haunt him forever.

"So, I guess social media is firing up with condemnation and hate." He stared out the window at the thick traffic.

"Enough to make me nervous. You've got sympathy from the hardcore fans but… We have to cancel the rest of the tour," she murmured. "The noise is too negative. You look like an insensitive asshat if you continue on as if nothing terrible has happened."

"We had six shows left." It could have been more, but he wished it had been fewer.

"Yep. That's well over a hundred thousand disappointed fans. And those are merely the ones who held tickets. It sucks." She hesitated. "You'll be thirty in less than eighteen months. I'm starting to think the time has come to tone down your bad-boy-gone-wild image."

She was right. Jesse didn't bother asking if his parents would be proud. They'd cashed out on his fame years ago. His dad now played golf with celebrities. His mom trained other stage parents and gave interviews about where they'd gone wrong with their only son. He hadn't talked to them in forever. But none of that mattered at the moment. Bottom line, Jesse wasn't proud of himself.

He hadn't been in a long time.

"We need a distraction," she told him. "You should start an anti-gun crusade."

Jesse shook his head. "Too political."

"What about a series of PSAs about suicide prevention?"

"Ryan didn't want to take his own life. He was simply too high to realize he shouldn't. Besides, doing either of those things will look like I know I should have done more."

Candia gave him a deflated sigh, then began chewing on her bottom lip as if sorting through the problem. "I'll keep working on solutions."

"While you think about my public image, find out how we can help the Harris girl's family, like providing funeral expenses or whatever else they need." He paused. "Have my lawyers work up a confidential settlement and set these folks up for life."

"But you had nothing to do with her death."

"All those parents know is that the last time their daughter walked out the door, she was coming to my concert. She'll never be home again because of the choices my bandmate made. They will never recover from that loss."

Candia got quiet. "I'll take care of it."

"Great. I appreciate you coming with me to talk to the rest of the band." They'd all been devastated but not stunned when he'd broken the news. "And when the police contact Ryan's parents and you get the details of his funeral, let me know."

She nodded. "Absolutely."

"Thanks. So…I guess you're canceling my appearances for a while?" When she nodded, the career-driven part of him grimaced. The rest of him exhaled in guilty relief. He hadn't had a day off in years.

"I'm afraid you won't be visiting Jimmy Fallon with this album," she quipped. "I think it's better if we proactively back out on these appearances for now, citing grief over the loss of your friend. We'll have an easier time rebooking in a couple of weeks, once this crap has died down."

"Wait. Maybe I should use those appearances to tell everyone that I had nothing to do with it." But he couldn't deny that on plenty of nights in the past, it could have been him—and everyone knew it. The fact that Maddy Harris had died in his hotel room simply splashed another stain on his already bad reputation. And it sure as hell made him feel shitty, too. What a waste of life…

"That's not what they want to hear. *'Rock Star Overdoses Underage Fan on Sex and Heroin'* makes for a juicier headline. Until the police finish their investigation and release the details, people will assume you had a hand in the incident."

He sighed. "So what do you want me to do?"

"I'm going to issue a statement expressing your grief and deepest apologies to the Harris family. You're going to disappear—way off the radar—until I say otherwise. No swanky resorts. No high-profile outings with Taylor Swift. And absolutely no intoxication. Think sober monk."

No one would ever believe that.

"I've got it." She snapped her fingers and excitement lit her eyes. "You can go to rehab."

Jesse scowled. "I'm not an addict."

"But it would look good. Repentant."

"It would also be pointless. Everyone goes to rehab and no one cares. No." He glared her way. "If I hole up, this dies down."

"All right," she said grudgingly as the limo stopped in front of the executive airport outside the city. "But I don't want to see a Twitter or Instagram pic of you for at least the next two weeks. Once we're back in L.A., hide out in your house. That should work. I'll tell you when it's safe to come out."

His ultra-contemporary house was decorated with every luxury and technological delight known to man, not to mention blessed with sick city and ocean views. But it had never felt like home. Despite the place being eight thousand square feet, Jesse couldn't imagine being cooped up there for the next fourteen days. It would only remind him of everything wrong with his life.

"Paparazzi know where I live. If I get on that plane with you and go to L.A., they'll figure it out. So will fans." Even now, he imagined that if he looked at his phone he'd find a full voicemail box and hundreds of text messages. He couldn't deal with anyone else's expectations right now when he'd done so poorly at meeting his own. "If you really want me to disappear, we'll have to come up with another plan."

"You're well known on every continent but Antarctica. The press would spot you almost anywhere you travel, especially if you take a security detail. They seem to have eyes and ears at every airport. I…" Candia huffed. "I need to think about this."

"I'll give it some brain power too, come up with a few ideas." Though he had no idea what to suggest, Jesse did know that what he'd done in the past—disappearing into the bottom of a bottle with some recreational blow and a woman under each arm—wasn't going to do a damn thing to clean up his image.

"Ideas?" She sounded as if that horrified her. "You? No."

"I'm a grown-ass man. And I've learned a few things over the years." He lowered his sunglasses and stared at her over the rims. "Go. You handle the press. I think I might know how to disappear."

When the driver opened the limo door, Candia grabbed her bag and turned to him. "You sure? Can I really trust you not to fuck this up?"

"Yeah. I know how much is on the line. Call me when the coast is clear."

* * * *

Jesse wiped his palms down the front of his jeans, then rang the doorbell. Hell, he didn't even know if Kimber was home. And that scary bastard she'd married—had it really been almost five years ago?— wouldn't be thrilled to see his wife's ex-fiancé, especially this late at night. If he was lucky, Deke Trenton would slam the door in his face. More likely, the big operative would try to beat the shit out of him.

After a gut-tightening moment, the porch light flipped on and the door swept open.

Deke towered in the doorway, a beefy forearm braced against the jamb, blue eyes raking him with a scathing glare. Then Kimber's husband sighed and looked over his shoulder, back into the living room. "Kitten, your personal Bieber has decided to drop in."

"Jesse?" He heard her familiar voice.

Deke stepped back, and she appeared in the doorway a moment later. Well, her pregnant belly edged into view. The rest of her followed an instant later. He hadn't talked to her in so long, he hadn't even known she was pregnant again. Didn't that make him feel even more like a shit?

Deke wrapped an arm around her—both a reminder and a warning. Jesse was relieved that seeing the man's hands on her no longer made him twenty kinds of jealous.

"Oh my gosh!" Kimber's hazel eyes widened as she pulled him into a quick hug. "You really are here."

Jesse held her in return for something slightly longer than a moment.

"Yeah. Sorry to drop by without calling." Clearly, he was intruding on their happy domestic scene.

"Not at all. Come in." She opened the door wider and stepped back.

He could have sworn he heard Deke growl. But the guy let Jesse enter. Now that he'd interrupted their evening, he'd talk fast, thank them, and be gone.

As he cleared the foyer, flashes of light told him the TV was on, but he suspected it had been muted because he didn't hear a sound coming from the box. Children's toys filled baskets and shelves around the room—balls, books, trucks, stuffed animals. Kimber had given birth to a son almost four years ago and was obviously about to be a mother again.

"Sit." She waved him over to the couch. "Can I get you something? Water? Coffee?"

Reluctantly, he sank into a chair, leaving the couch for the two of them. "No thanks. How are you?"

"Pregnant. It's a girl this time." She smoothed her hand over her distended belly with a serene smile. "I'm due at the end of next month. Otherwise, I'm fine."

"And you're on bed rest until then so you don't go into premature labor again. Feet up." Deke hustled her back to the sofa and lifted her lower legs and placed her heels on a pillow strategically positioned on top of the coffee table. Then the man pinned Jesse with a stare, shaking his head. "So I'm guessing this isn't a social call. Your buddy Ryan fucked up and bit it last night."

Kimber gasped, then elbowed her husband. "Deke!"

"Am I wrong?" Deke looked his way.

Jesse raked at his hair. He hated wearing it to his shoulders and filled with "product." The stylist he paid a small fortune for insisted it looked both cool and hot. Same with the scruff on his face. Sometimes he just wanted it all gone. "Nope. I wasn't there."

"*Access Hollywood* suggested something similar about an hour ago," she said.

"Which I don't watch," Deke cut in. "You came here for a reason. What do you need?"

Tugging at his ear, Jesse grimaced. These damn earrings weren't him, either. Crap, he shouldn't have come here. He didn't want to risk bringing the press down on them, especially if Kimber was having a difficult pregnancy. She didn't need the stress.

"Nothing." He stood. "You've got your hands full. I assume your son is in bed. And I… I'll figure it out."

"You need a place to go?" Deke barked.

Jesse opened his mouth to admit that's why he'd come, then he snapped it shut again. Deke's buddy Jack had some isolated cabin deep in a swamp, and it sure would come in handy about now. But Jesse hadn't done anything for himself since fame had hit—not kept his schedule, answered his calls, or styled his hair. Hell, he'd barely wiped his own ass. Simply rehabbing his image wouldn't cut it. As Candia had suggested, the time had come for him to change everything.

He was too damn unhappy to spend the rest of his life this way.

"No. I've got a place in mind," he lied. "Before I headed that way, I wanted to spend time with someone who..." *Knows I'm not the sort of man to corrupt and overdose a teenager.* But one of the last times he'd seen Kimber, she'd walked in to find him balls deep in an intoxicated, barely legal girl while chugging a fifth of bourbon. Deke must know that. "Someone who wouldn't bullshit me. Someone with a solid word of advice."

"Well..." Kimber wrinkled her brow in thought. "I've always told you that you have to decide what you want your life to be and make it happen."

Deke shook his head. "Kitten, I think he meant me."

When she glanced at him for confirmation, Jesse sent her a half grin. "Yeah, man to man. Or something like that."

His answer clearly surprised her. "Oh. Sure."

While it was no secret that Deke had never been a fan of his, and Jesse really had no right to ask for even a word from the man, he was thankful Kimber's hulk of a husband seemed willing to give it.

"Sit." He waited until Jesse complied. "I get it. Good times and fast women are easy to come by and hard to turn down." Deke sat back and took Kimber's hand. Though the overhead lights cast a glow on his golden hair, no one would ever mistake him for an angel. "But you've got to stop acting your age in rock star years."

"Rock star years?" Jesse frowned. What the hell was he talking about?

"Cut your age in half and add one." Deke cracked a smile.

Jesse shook his head. "I'm not fifteen."

"Then don't act like it. Life isn't about getting high or laid. Obviously, you've got an incredible career. It's your character everyone is questioning. Stop behaving like a douche. Start being a man. It's not complicated."

Well, he'd asked for it, and Deke had never been one to candy coat.

"I've been sober for a year. Actually, almost thirteen months."

"That's great!" Kimber praised.

The other man simply cocked his head and leveled him with a hard glance. "Women?"

Jesse didn't want to answer with Kimber in the room. His wandering penis had only been one of the reasons she'd left him. He hated to admit how little he'd changed since their breakup. "I'm no saint."

"Hmm," Deke mused. "Last bed partner?"

He hesitated. "A couple of cities ago."

"You remember her name?"

"No." Jesse grimaced.

"So she didn't mean anything to you?" Deke quizzed.

"Nothing."

"Then why did you do her?"

She'd been eager and pretty and willing and… "I don't know. I didn't have a reason not to."

"If you want your life to have meaning, you have to treat all the parts of your life as if they're meaning*ful*."

Deke's advice surprised Jesse. His words had almost sounded philosophical. Kimber's husband had always struck him as being long on intimidation and short on principles. Clearly, Jesse hadn't looked past the brawn.

His former fiancée wore a scowl. "Deke's right. When was the last time you wrote music? And recorded it? That used to mean everything to you."

He sucked in a breath and winced. "Longer than I'd like to admit."

"Your new album doesn't sound like you. It's great. Catchy and fun. Edgy. Clever." Kimber flushed. "That came out wrong. I know you can be fun and clever and all that. It's just…some of your best hits were soulful ballads about finding yourself and following your heart. You wrote those before you hit it big, and I haven't heard a song like that from you in forever."

She was right. Between the two of them, Jesse heard the message loud and clear that he'd lost his way, personally and professionally. This sabbatical away from the limelight had to be about becoming a whole new him. He couldn't wait. Getting the opportunity to change his partying, sex-god image—and himself—couldn't come soon enough.

"You're right. And I needed the honesty." Jesse stood. "Let me know when you have that baby. Thanks."

Chapter Two

Texarkana, Texas

"How have you not committed double murder?"

Bristol Reese stared into her beer, then glanced at her best friend. "They're not worth twenty-five to life. But don't think it hasn't crossed my mind."

Jayla scowled, her dark, expressive eyes both disapproving and dismissive. "Girl, that's restraint. He's a player and she's batty as hell."

"Which is why they deserve one another. I'm sure they'll have a short, miserable life together," she shot back, then chugged some of her brew, ignoring the clapping and laughter from the group gathered at the large table in the center of the restaurant.

Her friend's expression softened, her mocha skin glowing under the muted amber lights above the bar. "What about you? You gave that man sixteen months of your life. I really thought he intended to propose to you."

"I did, too. But I guess Hayden decided that Presleigh is better wife material."

Jayla snorted. "No, he thought having Miss Lafayette County on his arm would make him look like the shit with his buddies. That beauty pageant skank might look good in Victoria's Secret, but she's not you."

Bristol nodded. "Actually, I think that's something Hayden appreciates about her. And she's not a skank. It pains me to admit it, but she's sometimes sweet."

"She stole your man!"

"I don't think she had to try very hard," Bristol pointed out. "Hayden was dazzled by her short skirts and her adoration…and that was that."

Jayla pulled what she would have called her stank face. "His bitch ass needs to be taught a lesson."

Her friend was probably right, but Bristol had to take part of the blame. Her pride stung when she realized she'd buried her head in the sand and ignored her instincts about Hayden because she'd wanted him to be everything he wasn't—sweet, helpful, caring, capable of compromise. God, why was she so idealistic? A sweeping, romantic gesture bowled her heart over every time. She wanted Mr. Darcy to move heaven and earth to marry her, sought an Edward Lewis who was willing to conquer his fear of heights to rescue her so she could rescue him right back, hoped for her own Johnny Castle to tell her parents that nobody puts Bristol in a corner, ached for an Edward Cullen who knew his soul well enough to take one look at her and realize she was "The One."

She was a hopeless romantic, and it hadn't brought her a damn thing but misery.

"I'm not sure he's worth the effort." Bristol sighed.

"And Presleigh has no spine." Jayla was getting indignant on her behalf, slamming a fist on the bar.

"Another fact Hayden appreciates, I'm sure. I wouldn't conform enough for him. He always tried to change the way I dress, and all but bullied me to shut down my 'silly' business. He would have much preferred that I teach Sunday school at the church, maybe sell some Mary Kay on the side, and be blissfully happy to be Mrs. Hayden Vincent the third."

Jayla looked disgusted. "That's not you. You're too passionate about life to do nothing but keep a clean house, spit-polish up the kids for Christmas photos, and scrapbook your life away."

"Agreed." She drank more of her beer, then lowered the mug to the nearly empty bar with a sigh. "But you basically described Presleigh. Hell, maybe they are a perfect match."

"Ugh. He's falling for an empty package."

Bristol shrugged. "But he doesn't have much depth, either. I let myself be dazzled by a few roses and charming words from the most eligible guy in town. I mean, he's Lewisville, Arkansas's version of a Kennedy. I had a crush on him in high school something fierce. And he looked good in his football pants."

Jayla tilted her head. "I'll give you that."

"I appreciate you being mad on my behalf, but honestly...I'm more humiliated than heartbroken. I'm over him."

For the foreseeable future, no more entanglements of the heart. Flings only. If she kept the length of her relationships to a night—a weekend, tops—she couldn't make the same mistake again.

Bristol simply wished she didn't have to see Hayden and Presleigh together all the damn time. But in a town of twelve hundred people, avoiding them wouldn't be easy. Even if she moved away, she'd come home to visit and run into them eventually.

"A toast," Corey, one of Hayden's football friends from high school said, standing in front of the rest of the gathering. "Raise your glasses, everyone. To Presleigh, the most beautiful girl in Lafayette County. May you always follow your heart and be happy. To Hayden... Cheers, man. You're one lucky bastard."

As the crowd laughed, Bristol looked on with a sigh...then spotted her mother bustling over, her Pepto-Bismol pink suit looking more suited to Easter Sunday services than an engagement party.

"You're being rude," her mother chastised. "This is Presleigh's event, and you're sitting at the bar, sulking. Come give her your love and support. After all, she is your sister."

Bristol tightened her grip on her mug. "I closed my restaurant early and drove forty-five minutes down the road to celebrate her upcoming nuptials to the man who dumped me for her. I think the fact that I'm here at all is enough."

"You sound bitter," her mother tsked, her hair not blowing at all as the air conditioner kicked on.

She wasn't. She and Hayden hadn't been a good match, and she hadn't wanted to admit it. In truth, he'd done her a favor by falling for someone else. Bristol just wished that someone hadn't been her younger sister. At nineteen, Presleigh was too young to get married and too pampered to know what the word compromise meant.

"Mama, leave it. Please. I'm not making waves. I'm still speaking to her. And to him. Anything more will take time."

Her mother frowned. "At least come sit with the group. Food will be served soon, and the rest of the family is asking questions."

Because keeping up appearances with her Aunt Jean, a distant cousin, and the rest of the townsfolk was far more important than any potential heartbreak or misery her own daughter may have suffered.

Beside her, Jayla rolled her eyes. She and Linda Mae Reese had never gotten along. Her best friend had always sworn that her mother favored

Presleigh. Bristol had never experienced that as vividly as she was right now.

"We'll be there in a few minutes, Mama. I'm just waiting for a friend." Maybe the others would be done eating before she had to admit that her "friend" hadn't shown up—what a shame—and she joined the party as it wound down for the evening.

"Who?" Her mother frowned. "We didn't invite anyone else, Bristol."

In her mom's vernacular, that meant that Bristol asking someone new to join the party without her knowledge bordered on unacceptable.

Jayla gave Linda Mae a sweet-as-pie smile. "Her new boyfriend."

Bristol whirled on her barstool. "Are you crazy?"

What the hell was she going to do when no new man showed up except look more pathetic?

Her pal gave her an apologetic grimace. "It slipped out."

Quickly, Bristol scanned the few men nearby to see if any might be suitable fake boyfriend material. Maybe she could bribe him with a few drinks to play nice for an hour. But no guy fit the bill. Predictably, most folks in a restaurant near the five p.m. mark were at least old enough to be social security eligible or were married with children.

"Oh." Her mother reared back, obviously surprised. "I didn't know you were seeing someone. Who is he? Where did you meet? What does he do? Where does he live?"

The more her mother asked questions, the more suspicious she sounded—with good reason. It wasn't as if Lewisville had a huge pool of eligible bachelors, and Bristol didn't make the trip west to Texarkana often.

She shot Jayla a glare. Her friend shrugged in silent apology. She appreciated Jayla wanting to prevent her mother from continuing the bitter-hag routine, but this lie simply didn't help.

"Mama…" Bristol sighed, knowing she needed to swallow a choking bite of humble pie and admit that she was totally single. But damn, she wished she didn't have to.

Behind her, she heard a shuffle and turned to see an absolutely gorgeous guy emerge from the shadows. His tight black tank framed an amazing set of muscled shoulders, one of which was covered by a tribal tattoo. He had a strong jaw, wore a black skullcap and a pair of expensive-looking sunglasses, along with a smile that made her breath catch.

When he removed the shades to stare at her, his dark eyes danced with amusement. "Hi, honey. Sorry I'm late."

* * * *

Jesse knew he should have resisted butting in, but the cute little brunette had clearly been through hell with her sister and the ex-asshat. Her mother's haranguing only seemed to make her sink down on her barstool more, as if she wanted to escape. He knew what it was like to have shit coming at him from all directions. That lesson felt particularly fresh now.

He had sneaked a peek at the entertainment news on his smart phone when he'd wandered into town a few hours ago…and wished he hadn't. If he could go back in time and stop Ryan from tragically ending two lives, he'd be eternally grateful. Sadly, a miracle wasn't in the cards for him, but he kind of hoped the girl at the bar saw him as one. She wasn't crying in her beer yet, but if he couldn't give her some breathing room soon, she absolutely might.

When he spoke, her green eyes, tucked under the sun-kissed fringe of her bangs, bounced from the bar, up to his face. She blinked, stared. Jesse worried that covering his shorn hair, shaving the scruff, removing his earrings, and not wearing leather wouldn't be enough to disguise him. He knew damn well he'd taken a big, impulsive risk by showing himself in public—but who could resist a dive called Bubba Oink's Bone Yard?— and jumping in to Bristol's situation. Thankfully, he didn't see recognition on her face, merely confusion.

"I'm not too late, am I?" he prompted.

She swallowed, and her pretty African-American friend discreetly nudged her ribs with an elbow. The brunette slid off the stool. "Ah…no. We haven't eaten yet."

"What's your name, young man? My daughter hasn't mentioned you." Her mother, who had a serious case of helmet hair, sent him a frown somewhere between puzzled and disapproving.

He stuck out a hand and improvised. "My name is James, ma'am. Most of my friends call me Jamie. Nice to meet you."

Her mother took his hand. Her soft skin felt cold. "James. I'm Linda Mae."

"I'm Jayla," Bristol's friend added with a friendly handshake. "So glad I finally get to meet you."

"Pleasure." He nodded at the women, then took the pretty brunette's hand in his. "It's good to see you, Bristol."

Surprise widened her eyes even more. He liked the way she wore her emotions on her face, the way freckles dusted her nose, the way her pouty lower lip shimmered under the lights.

"Um...you, too, Jamie." She sent him a stilted smile.

Linda Mae shook her head suspiciously, then huffed back to the others.

"We should join the party," her friend suggested and grabbed her by the elbow, hauling her toward the gathering. She gazed past Bristol to him with a wink. "Thanks for joining us."

He grinned back and followed. "You're welcome."

The long table around which everyone else sat looked fairly cramped, and Jesse didn't think Bristol wanted to get cozy with these folks anyway. So he pulled up seats at the empty table directly behind it. He placed Bristol between him and her friend, then looped a casual arm around the back of her chair, brushing her long ponytail as he did. He'd enjoy his knight-in-shining-armor routine for an evening, then he and Bristol could have an amicable "breakup" before he continued down the road in search of somewhere to spend the next couple of weeks. But for tonight, she'd have a reason to thumb her nose at her mother and sister.

On the far side of the party's table, a blonde wearing too much makeup and a gaudy engagement ring made googly eyes at a twerp with light brown hair and a condescending expression. Bristol had dated *him*?

The rest of the party sent him glances ranging from curious to suspicious. He waved. "Hi, everyone. I'm Jamie, Bristol's new boyfriend."

After a brief round of introductions, he settled back into his chair and watched his supposed new squeeze. She was built on the petite side, but he'd already noticed when she rose from her barstool that her jeans hugged the curves of her really pert ass. The pretty little thing also had a noteworthy rack.

She glanced his way, then leaned in to Jayla, speaking softly. "Did you set this up? Hire him or something?"

The other woman shook her head. "No. He just appeared. Like a fairy godfather."

"Without the glitter and wings," Jesse quipped in low tones.

"Seriously?" She swiveled her gaze in his direction. "Why would you help me?"

"Because you needed it, and I can't resist a damsel in distress." He flashed her a smile filled with the dimples that had been getting him laid since he turned fifteen. He probably shouldn't but he hoped they were working now.

Bristol frowned, looking uncertain. Did she wish he hadn't butted in?

He leaned back to give her space. "Do you want me to go?"

She chewed on her bottom lip and stared as if trying to figure him out. "Who are you?"

A splash of adrenaline spiked his bloodstream. Had she recognized him after all?

"I'm Jamie." Well, that was his cousin's name, but he'd at least turn around if someone shouted it. Hopefully. He leaned closer and whispered in her ear. "I'm not a crazed rapist or ax murderer, if that's what you're worried about. I overheard your dilemma and decided to help. I just want to see you smile, okay?"

"Everything all right?" a male voice called from the next table.

The groom-to-be tried to stare him down, narrowing his eyes to something he probably thought resembled a Hollywood action hero's most intimidating glare. Jesse tried not to laugh.

"Great," he assured the dickwad.

Bristol's sister latched onto her fiancé's arm and looked up at him as if she sought all the answers of the universe in his eyes. Jesse didn't have anything against love or adoration. He didn't know much about them, but he didn't think her insipid expression was a good representation of either.

"Is that guy bothering you?" Bristol's ex asked her, nodding his way.

Jesse tensed, waiting to see what she'd say. She glanced away from the fidiot and over to him again. She tucked her hand in his and squeezed. "Why would you think that? I'm great, Hayden."

"She's just put out that I'm late," Jesse lied smoothly. "Carry on."

Hayden did so reluctantly, telling everyone at the gathering about the moment he'd realized he was in love with her sister over punch and cake, right after Presleigh risked herself to rescue the neighbor's kid from an angry hive of bees.

"Is he talking about Ben Bob?" When Bristol nodded, Jayla rolled her eyes. "C'mon now. That kid threw rocks at the hive because he wanted to see what the bees would do."

"Yep. He even admitted that."

Jayla frowned, as if remembering an annoying but key fact. "Didn't that happen at *your* birthday party?"

"It did." Bristol nodded with an acid smile.

So Hayden had thrown her over for her vapid sister when he'd come to celebrate her big day? "What a raving douche."

"You got that right," Jayla put in.

While Jesse couldn't deny that he'd pulled some dick moves when he had been briefly engaged to Kimber, that had been years ago, when he had been young, intoxicated, and stupid. Back then, he'd believed the world owed him a good time.

How had anybody tolerated him?

"Thanks for that assessment, babe," Bristol tossed back at him, wearing an intriguing hint of a grin.

"If hearing me diss your ex makes you happy, I'll be glad to do it more."

Her grin widened, almost becoming a full-blown smile.

Before Jesse could coax one out of her, the waitstaff began bringing everyone glasses of sweet tea and trays full of beef brisket sandwiches, coleslaw, baked beans, and bread. Bottles of wine followed. Hayden called for a bucket of beer. People dug in, conversation ensued, and the bride and groom looked at each other as if they couldn't wait to be alone. Jesse wondered if they realized how incredibly insensitive they were being. Probably not. Even if they did, Jesse suspected they wouldn't care if they hurt Bristol. Obviously, they'd disregarded her feelings some time ago.

Thankfully, the restaurant began piping in music, a kind of modern country tune that Jesse didn't hear often but liked. He eyed Bristol as she bounced in her chair to the beat. Her gesture looked completely unconscious, as if she didn't expect anyone would be watching her. He kind of found it adorable.

When the waiter began taking the food away, she'd barely touched hers. Instead, she peered at him as if he was a riddle she needed to solve. The intelligence on her face, coupled with an unconsciously sultry thing she had going on, piqued his interest. Blood rushed south. Against his better judgment, his cock stood up and saluted her.

Shit, he'd jumped into this situation to help—nothing more. He'd just rolled into town and wasn't sure what to do with himself. He hadn't cast himself in the role of her boyfriend in the hopes that she'd let him fuck her.

Everyone around them was laughing and imbibing. The engaged couple kissed again. Bristol tried not to look at them. Jesse wanted to wring their necks.

"Walk with me?" he leaned closer and asked in her ear.

She turned his way, her big green eyes snaring his gaze. "Where?"

"I don't know. I've never been to this place. Where can we talk without technically leaving the party?"

She paused, then turned to Jayla. "Will you distract my mother for a few minutes, pretty please?"

"You did *not* just ask me to do that." Her bestie crossed her arms over her chest and gave her a glare full of attitude.

"I'll make you a whole batch of peanut butter blossom cookies," she wheedled.

Suddenly, Jayla gave her a dazzling smile. "Deal."

"I think I got played," Bristol told him with a fond shake of her head.

"I'd say so." He held out his hand.

She tucked her cell phone in her pocket, leaving her purse with her friend, then she placed her hand in his outstretched palm as they strolled the perimeter of the restaurant/bar. "So…what made you jump in? Did I look like a sad spinster, so you decided to end my singledom for a night?"

"No. I'm a sucker for engagement parties. Can't you tell? I saw all the white balloons with the cute pictures of the bride and groom attached and I couldn't resist. If I'm lucky, maybe we can catch another sappy speech and drink some terrible champagne."

She sent him a skeptical glare. "Have you ever been to an engagement party?"

"Not since my neighbor's daughter married an alpaca farmer. I was twelve," he admitted.

Bristol laughed, and Jesse loved hearing the light, lyrical sound. That giggle was a music all its own. "Made a big impact on you, huh?"

"The cake did. But the marriage lasted about as long as I think your sister's will."

"It took me longer to decorate the 'save the date' cookies she asked me for tonight than the whole marriage will, I suspect. The wedding is next month. Mama wanted her to be a June bride. Presleigh isn't ready to be anyone's wife."

"And he's no Prince Charming."

She nodded. "There is that."

"Why did you date him?"

"That's a good question." Bristol hesitated. "He found me after I broke my ankle and took me to the doctor."

"You felt as if you owed him?" Jesse asked.

"No. I liked him—or I thought I did. But that was before I actually knew him."

"How did you get hurt?" Even in the dimming light, he saw the flush in her cheeks, and Jesse sensed a story. "Okay, 'fess up."

"Well, I bought this aerobics video and I was trying it out but…"

"Your ankle snapped, did it? Were you doing some crazy *Insanity* shit?"

She twirled a section of her hair around one finger and looked anywhere but at him. "Um, no."

"So…what were you up to?"

Biting back a smile, she sent him a coy glance. "It was supposed to be pole dancing but I didn't have a pole, so I used a column in my apartment. I didn't know it was hollow and wouldn't hold me. I landed wrong and…it was embarrassing."

He gave a hearty laugh. "I don't mean to make light of your pain, but you have to admit that—"

"No, it totally sounds funny. And if anyone could have seen it, I'll bet it would have been hysterical."

Maybe, but he'd bet that before her fall, he'd have found her sexy as hell. "So he took you to the hospital?"

She nodded. "Yep. He also brought me roses while they set the cast. Then he filled my prescriptions and took me home. He even tried to pet my cat, Shakespurr."

"That's what you named your cat?"

"Yeah, he's a feline so he's clever and creative. And just like the Bard himself, before I had Shakespurr fixed he liked older women."

"Right." Jesse enjoyed her sense of humor and quick wit. He wondered how many of the women he'd taken to bed over the years he might have liked if he'd bothered to get to know them. Probably none. This one seemed really different. "So you decided you liked him because he tried to pet your pussy?"

She tsked at him and sent him an annoyed glare, hands on her hips. But the fact that she was about a foot shorter, coupled with the smile she couldn't repress, took all the starch out of her censure.

"That's not all. Hayden also told me that he had a crush on me in high school."

"And you fell for him?"

Bristol heaved a long sigh. "Totally. I sound like an idiot."

Jesse didn't like hearing her put herself down when she'd done nothing wrong. "No. You sound like a woman who trusted the wrong guy because you wanted to believe the best about him."

"I really did."

Now she sounded sad, and he wanted to turn her frown into another smile. "Since you've been so honest, I guess I'll tell you something true." He squeezed her hand. "I saw you sitting on the barstool talking to Jayla and thought you were beautiful. If you've once thought you're not simply because the ex-jackass tossed you over for your younger sister, trust me. It's not you; it's him. I can already tell you're way smarter. I also suspect you're a better human being. So if he made you feel lousy, forget it. I've traveled all over the world and met a lot of women. You seem pretty awesome to me."

She blushed again. "Thanks."

"Like I said, just being honest."

A comfortable lull fell between them, and Jesse finally scanned his surroundings. He'd played a number of places with this vibe when he'd first started singing. It hadn't taken long before a random YouTube video had brought him to the attention of record producers. He'd been too nervous to appreciate the valuable learning experience and too young to join the revelry that would inevitably happen here later. Right now, a band dragged in their instruments and readied themselves for their Saturday night set.

Besides maturity and experience, the other thing that made his trip to this joint different was the fact that he held Bristol's hand in his. He liked the simple touch, liked knowing she was there with him step by step. She didn't have any expectations that he'd find the nearest room away from his screaming public to get in her panties. Bristol seemed perfectly content to simply be with him.

Conversely, the fact that she wasn't squealing to sleep with *the* Jesse McCall really made him want her. Or was there just something about her that did it for him?

"So…since you saved me from social hell tonight, are you expecting money?"

If she only knew how much he didn't need it. "Nope."

"Sex?" She quirked a brow at him.

Jesse couldn't help but smile. "I wouldn't turn it down…"

"Oh, yeah?" Her smile dipped. "And you're not interested in Presleigh?"

"God, no. She's pretty in that plastic way, like a Barbie doll. Sure, she's cute and has a nice bod. But I've met a million girls like her. She's not interesting."

"And I am?" Bristol quizzed, looking a bit skeptical.

"So far, yeah."

"You don't really know me," she pointed out.

"Fair enough. But you seem real. Unlike your sister, it's pretty clear you didn't spend all afternoon preening in front of the mirror and dressing for attention."

"What does that mean? Maybe I did."

"I guess that messy ponytail with the chunk that didn't make it up—

nice scrunchie, by the way—was on purpose. And who wants to wear a skirt so short that a stiff breeze could reveal your underwear when you could go the rumpled jeans route? Much sexier. And that patch of flour on your neck here." He swept his fingers over the spot and felt her pulse jump. "Hmm, honey. It's a turn-on."

She gave a tsk of self-disgust and swiped at the flour, then dragged the elastic band covered in pink polka-dotted fabric from her hair. The multi-hued brown strands bounced past her shoulders and brushed her arms, the ends a shade much closer to blond. It wasn't any sort of ombre dye job, simply a natural byproduct of the sun. Her tresses framed her delicate face.

"Okay, so I'm not *Vogue* ready."

"But like I said, you are pretty, no matter what you're wearing," he told her. "You know, since I'm your boyfriend for the evening, I should know more about you. I mean, in case people ask? At least the vitals."

"That's a point. My mother may have paused her interrogation, but she'll be back." She seemed to gather her thoughts. "I'm twenty-four, my middle name is Alexa. My dad died when I was ten. We used to bake together when I was a kid. I dropped out of college in my sophomore year to start a little coffeehouse in my hometown called *Sweet Cinns*. Making ends meet each month is touch and go, but I love what I do and wouldn't change a thing. What about you?"

"I'm still trying to find myself. I got a GED at sixteen. I had this crazy idea, but it didn't work out the way I thought. So…right now, I'm seeing the country and trying to figure out where to go next. Where's your hometown?" He changed the subject before she could ask him for details.

"Lewisville. That's in Arkansas, about thirty miles east. You've never heard of it."

"I haven't," he admitted.

"It's a tiny town, so small that we had to come here to find a restaurant big enough for the party."

"Do you have a lot of competition in the restaurant biz there?"

"Well, it's not like Starbucks has come to town, so that helps. But we also don't have a morning rush hour. I'd love to have cars wrapped around the building, but it isn't equipped with a drive-thru. No other place in town is open for breakfast or makes everything from scratch. I don't stay open for dinner because I can't compete with Burge's Pit Bar-B-Q or Scooter's Pizza Shack."

He nodded as they meandered closer to the band. "Wise business decision. I'll bet your goodies are delicious. I'd love a taste."

His voice had gone low and husky, and Jesse wondered if she'd heard it.

She raised her gaze to him, lashes fluttering flirtatiously. "Is that right? Well, my hot buns are fabulous."

"I have no doubt they are." He winked. When she giggled, he wished he could stay around long enough to take a bite of whatever she offered.

A few moments later, the collection of musicians grabbed their instruments and started playing a lively contemporary country love song with a three-four meter. It wasn't like anything he played in his vault of songs.

"Dance with me?" he asked, stopping at the edge of the floor and drawing her closer.

"You waltz?"

Not really. "Sure."

Mostly, he just wanted to hold her close.

She bit her lip. "I'm not much of a dancer."

"I'm pretty decent. I'll go easy on you. Say yes." He skimmed a palm down her back.

She exhaled, her breath shaky. Her stare never left his face. "Okay. They're your toes."

"You'll do great."

Jesse took her hand in his and brought her closer. Every one of her curves seemed to align perfectly with him, each contour fitting to his like pieces of a puzzle. That sounded cheesy, even in his own head, but he'd never been more aware of a woman's every dip and swell, of his heart racing simply because she stood near and their palms touched. He wasn't at the eighth grade formal, slow-dancing with a girl for the very first time. He'd long ago lost track of how many women he'd slept with. But she made everything seem new again.

Were his palms actually sweating?

They fell in time to the music together, Jesse mimicking the sort of waltz his grandparents used to dance. Bristol seemed a bit stiff at first, but with every step she relaxed more into his arms.

"Where did you learn to dance?" she asked.

He couldn't say that his very first manager had hired dance instructors to work with him to perfect his on-stage moves and that, more recently, he'd hired a "male entertainer" to show him how to make his moves sexier. Instead, he opted for something he could tell her.

"My grandparents owned an Arthur Murray dance studio. I spent my summers there. When I was thirteen, I thought it would be the happening place to pick up girls, so I paid attention. I learned a lot."

"I'll bet you were smooth even back then."

"I thought I was." He smiled at her. "I see the pictures now and think 'dork in braces.'"

She laughed. "I can't imagine it."

"True story."

Because he wasn't digging even the small bit of distance between them, Jesse flattened his palm to her back, sliding down to the sway in her spine, bringing her petite frame and sweet curves even closer. He didn't usually have any trouble controlling his cock. Now it had a mind of its own, and he ached to slide all of her against every inch of him too badly to care if she felt that.

When he arched into her, she gasped, then flattened herself against him. The friction as they swayed together blew his mind. She glanced up at him, and he curled a finger under her chin to bring her face beneath his. He really had to restrain himself from grabbing her ass. Public displays didn't bother him but that sort of thing might bug her. And he wasn't supposed to be drawing attention to himself.

"If you don't want me to kiss you, say something now."

"I...I can't."

Jesse eased back, trying not to let the surprisingly visceral disappointment consume him. "You can't let me kiss you?"

"No, I can't say anything."

His entire body tensed. He wanted to throw her to the ground and get inside her in the next thirty seconds. Sure he liked sex. Loved it. But this compulsion to take off Bristol's clothes and make her scream out his name seemed way beyond any normal urge.

He took her face in his hands. God, she was so small in his grip. Delicate. Lovely. Her stare clung to him, her green eyes so open and earnest. She wasn't playing a game, wasn't merely interested in him because of who he was. She seemed to like *him*.

Now was a really crappy time to decide that he seriously liked a girl. Jesse knew he should walk away. But Deke had advised him to make all the parts of his life meaningful. Bristol Reese might be the most meaningful thing he'd felt in years.

Chapter Three

Bristol fought to catch her breath. When Jamie cradled her face and looked into her eyes as if nothing in his life meant more than this kiss, an electric spark had sizzled down her spine. The answering jolt darkened his hungry stare.

She hadn't felt important to anyone since her father. She wasn't unhappy being alone, but her ill-fated relationship with Hayden had taught her that she couldn't play second best anymore. Looking back, she saw that he'd always gravitated to Presleigh. Too often, he'd been happy to forego an evening with her to have dinner with her mother and sister. Jamie could care less that her beauty queen sibling was anywhere in the building.

"Good. I'm going to kiss you." His voice sounded husky, rough. His grip on her tightened as if he didn't want to let her go. "I'm going to make you open to me so I can taste every corner of your mouth. I want to know what it feels like when you melt against me and moan in surrender."

Her heart picked up speed until she could hear its beating in her ears. "Sure of yourself, aren't you?"

He shook his head. "I'm banking on the hope that this pull I'm feeling toward you isn't one-sided. The way you're looking at me says it's not. If I'm wrong, tell me."

"You're not," she breathed. "This is crazy. We met an hour ago." But she still felt as if she knew him in some weird way on a soul-deep level. Jamie made her hormones swirl and did something she couldn't quite classify to her heart. Walking away from him now simply because they hadn't had a requisite date at Chili's before sharing a movie didn't make sense. It didn't have any bearing on whether they slipped into bed.

Hadn't she vowed earlier to have flings? Jamie seemed as if he'd qualify as the perfect one.

He leaned closer, his gaze focused on hers as his lids shut. Her breathing stopped. Her heartbeat stuttered, then lurched. Bristol wanted to know how being close to him would feel. He wasn't her "type" and that didn't seem to matter at all.

"Bristol?" She'd know that sharp voice anywhere.

"Yes, Mama?"

"Hayden and Presleigh have a few words to say to everyone. And she'd like you to pass out the cookies."

"Damn it," she muttered under her breath. When Jamie smiled down at her, his hands still cupping her face, his warmth went a long way to squelching her disappointment. He wasn't letting her mother ruin their first kiss. She wouldn't either. "I'll be right there."

"And Aunt Jean wants to know what she's doing wrong with her chocolate sheet cake."

"I'll bet she tried to use two-percent instead of buttermilk again," she murmured to Jamie. "Sure thing. I'll be right there."

The sound of her mother's heels clicking away was a relief.

"Does she do that a lot?" he asked.

"Interrupt my love life. No. I don't have much of one."

"Excuse me while I have a Neanderthal moment and tell you I'm glad to hear that." He chuckled. "I meant does she try to direct you."

Bristol rolled her eyes. "All the time. She's from a really old-fashioned family. If you're not a wife and mother, you're not really an adult. There's no such thing as being a single woman who can look after herself in this neck of the woods."

"I'll bet you have an independent streak."

"Always have," she said wryly. "But I need to get back or she'll badger me."

"Then let's go." He took her hand and led her toward the others.

"Thanks for not bailing."

He scoffed comically. "I'm your boyfriend for the night. What kind of asshole would that make me to dump you in the middle of a party?"

"Someone more similar to Hayden than I'd like."

He laughed. "Not the image I'm going for."

As they reached the gathering, Presleigh was still clinging to Hayden as if he was her sun and moon. He flashed a smile down at her, as if he wanted everyone to know that he was enamored with his bride-to-be. Bristol had once seen that expression directed at her, and she wondered what her younger sister would do if someone new caught his eye.

Presleigh spotted her and smiled. "Thank you, everyone, for coming. Invitations are in the mail, but Bristol also made delicious cookies and frosted them with our wedding date. She's so clever." Her sister sent her an earnest expression. "In fact, she's one of the most important people in my life. Bris, I'm hoping you'll be my maid of honor."

Bristol felt her eyes widen and tried to keep the horror off her face. Wasn't it enough that she'd given Presleigh her man and baked her engagement cookies? Now she had to stand next to her sister as she married the man who had once been hers?

"Are you fucking kidding me?" Jamie muttered under his breath.

"I thought you wanted me to bake your cake." Bristol didn't know what else to say.

"I do," Presleigh assured with an excited shake of her head. "But you've always stood next to me in childhood. I want you to stand beside me as I become a wife."

"It would mean a lot to both of us," Hayden added.

Was this really happening? "Didn't you already ask your friend Shea?"

"Yeah, but she and Corey"—she pointed at Hayden's friend—"had that ugly breakup. Now they won't even speak two words to each other. I finally decided that it was fate telling me that you should be the one to stand beside me. Mama is going to walk me down the aisle since Daddy isn't here. Please... It will be perfect."

What a lovely piece of emotional blackmail, wheedling in front of almost everyone she knew so that she'd look like a bitch if she refused. Never mind that she was apparently second choice. "Um..."

"I've already picked out a dress and ordered it. It will fit perfectly and look fantastic. Please..."

It would probably look awful since she and Presleigh had polar opposite tastes. Bristol took a deep breath. It didn't matter. As Daddy had always said, family was family—and they came first. As much as she didn't want to do this, Bristol also didn't want to start a family feud over her pride.

"All right. I'll do it."

Jamie scoffed beside her. Yeah, she would have liked a graceful way out of this mess, too. But this commitment would last one day, over and done. Then she would step back and let Hayden and her sister live their lives.

"Thanks, Bris." Presleigh looked as if she was going to tear up. "It means so much to me."

Bristol smiled and tried to make it look genuine. "You're welcome. On that note, the cookies are in the storage container in front of you if you'd like to pass them out."

"They're your cookies. Don't you want to?" Her sister looked confused.

Her ego could pass up the stroke of hearing the cookies were pretty. A sugary shortbread topped with white icing and black piping to draw the June calendar, the treats had come out well.

"I'm good." Bristol shook her head. "Jamie and I are going now."

If he seemed surprised by her proclamation, he didn't show it.

When her mother scowled in disapproval, Jamie acted as if her sour expression didn't exist. "She promised to spend some time with me since we're still getting to know one another." He reached across the table and snagged a cookie out of the red plastic container. "Nice to meet you all."

With that, he grabbed her purse from the table and led her out of the restaurant, taking a big bite of the pastry as they hit the door. Just outside, he stopped completely and moaned. "Oh, my god. Are you kidding me? This is a foodgasm. Amazing."

She grinned up at him. "Did you doubt me?"

"If I ever did, I won't do it again." He moaned once more. "I understand why Jayla manipulated you for cookies. I may have to learn strategy from her."

He wouldn't be around that long since she only did temporary relationships now, but that was all right. He could flirt all he wanted. "How about an ooey-gooey cinnamon roll? They're what I'm known for. I'll make you a pan…" She took a deep breath. "If you're still with me come morning."

He froze altogether again—everything except his eyes. They came absolutely alive. Dark, focused, demanding as he scanned her face to see if she was serious. God, he really was hot. She couldn't wait to see him without the black skullcap, without the clothes that hid what she felt sure would be a breath-stealingly hard body. Not to mention that he was funny and nice and…seemingly on the same wavelength as her.

"Your place?" he asked.

"Is that a yes?"

He grabbed her shoulders, pressing their foreheads together. "That's a hell yes. Lead the way. I'll follow you on my bike."

Bristol didn't wait for Jamie to change his mind. She dug her keys from her purse and leveled him with a sexy stare full of come-hither. "Keep up."

"I will," he vowed. "Then once I have you naked and under me, I'll get deep inside and fill you up. You won't have a single regret."

Bristol refused to regret anything. She was determined they would make this a night to remember.

She hopped in her car, and he followed her on some sleek black-and-chrome motorcycle. Watching him lean over the machine, his thighs hugging the bike as it roared and purred, seeing him handle it with an enticing male grace and agility, totally revved her desire. She'd always dated seemingly good guys...who never turned out to be quite as good as she'd believed. Jamie was all bad boy.

Bristol couldn't wait.

A few miles shy of Lewisville, her phone rang. Jayla's contact appeared, and she answered the call right away. "Hey!"

"I tried to save you, but your mama wouldn't listen."

"Save me?" Her stomach tightened with worry. "Uh oh. What does that mean?"

"She wants you to come to dinner on Tuesday night—and to bring Jamie."

"No. Absolutely not. He's my Saturday night fling."

"Well, your mama thinks he's your new man."

"And whose fault is that?" Bristol groused. "So he and I will have to break up before then."

Jayla got quiet. That was never a good sign.

"Spit it out. What's the issue?"

"Your mama invited half of Lewisville, and the townsfolk are starting to think that you're not interested in hanging onto a man."

Bristol gripped the steering wheel. "I'm not—not anymore."

"But you know how they think. You're either a good girl looking to get married or a ho-bag who doesn't deserve their business."

Shock pinged through Bristol. "Seriously?" Then she thought it through and cursed. "Never mind. I know it's true. So basically, I have to look ready to pair up with Jamie until death do us part before he dumps me horribly—much later—so I can win their sympathy or else no one will buy another mushroom omelet or peach cobbler from me, right?"

"That's pretty much how it is."

This debacle would probably be crazy to anyone who didn't live in a tiny town. But here, where everyone knew everybody and their business, Jayla's reminder was irrefutable.

"Damn it." Bristol shook her head. "I'll deal with it. Thanks for the warning."

"Thanks for not shooting the messenger."

Jayla rang off, and Bristol tried to decide exactly how to plead or bribe Jamie into coming to dinner on Tuesday night. Since it sounded as if he was between jobs, hopefully it wouldn't be a problem. Normally, that would bother her since she preferred to date guys who were gainfully employed. But she wasn't planning a long-term relationship with Jamie, just sex.

She glanced in the rearview mirror. He still sat about twenty feet off her back bumper as they headed east on Highway 82. Maybe she could sweet talk the man or feed him incredible desserts to make him stay through Tuesday. Or tie him to her bed. That had appeal. Though she'd like it better if he tied her down.

And if the townsfolk found out she fantasized about that, they'd absolutely die.

Still, she imagined what she and Jamie might do together, her autopilot keeping her compact on the highway. When she looked up again, they were cruising into Lewisville. Along the town's main drag, on the corner, she saw her shop and pulled into the parking lot behind the building as the sun dipped toward the horizon. Lewisville looked its best this time of day. Even then, it still appeared older, sometimes a bit neglected. Most children raised here left the moment they could. Bristol wondered why she'd stayed. Concern for her mother and sister? Memories of Daddy? Or being too afraid to leave everything she'd ever known?

Shaking off the thought, she stepped out of her car, purse on her shoulder, as Jamie climbed off his bike.

"Cute little town," he said.

"Small."

"Quaint," he corrected.

"That's a nice way of putting it." She gestured to her place. "Want the tour?"

"Sure."

She let them both in the back door. She mostly kept supplies here, along with a small office in the corner. Flipping on lights, she led him into her kitchen, which sparkled—just as it did every day after the close of business. Her industrial oven and mixer gleamed. Pristine stainless countertops covered the length of two walls, waiting for her to create the next yummy treat. She'd had to get a loan from a bank in Texarkana since the town's one financial institution had refused to loan funds to a "kid," but she'd done it on her own. And she was proud.

"So this is where the dough happens?" He winked.

"Yeah. And up front here…" Bristol directed him through the next door and into the front of the shop with its display cases and bistro tables. "This is the customer area. I can only seat twenty since the building is a converted brownstone and this room is the former parlor. But I'm proud of it."

Jamie looked around, seeming to take in every nuance. His eyes gleamed with appreciation. "It's got a lot of charm. Most places I go have none."

She frowned. "What has you traveling so much?"

"Gotta make a buck." He shrugged. "So do you live somewhere near your shop?"

She wondered what he did for a living but got the feeling he didn't want to talk about it. And did she really need to know if they were simply going to have a fling? "Upstairs."

Maybe it didn't seem smart to take a stranger home, but instinct told her Jamie wasn't dangerous. Besides, her family and friends knew who she'd gone home with. Jayla would no doubt check on her.

Bristol took Jamie's hand and guided him back to her stock room and to the staircase along one wall she and Jayla had restored to its original gleaming wood, just like the floors.

Together, she and Jamie charged up to her apartment, and she unlocked the door. As it creaked open, the last golden rays of the day illuminated her rustic chic space—the cozy white sofa, the glass table built on whiskey barrels, the braided rug under her grandmother's dining room table.

He glanced around, then cocked his head in thought. "It's you."

She smiled and shut the door behind them, flipping on the overhead lights. "Yeah?"

"Comfortable, happy, unvarnished. I like it."

"Thanks." He seemed to get her, and that did Bristol's heart a world of good. Hayden had hated this place. He liked things grander and more formal, not an eclectic grouping of her favorite things. He called antiques "recycled junk." "But you didn't come all the way to Lewisville to comment on my decor, right?"

"No." He turned to her, his hands suddenly engulfing her hips, his stare drilling down into her eyes. "I did not."

"So what did you come to do?" she challenged.

He gave her a panty-melting grin as he pulled her closer, fitting her flush against his body where she could feel every inch of him. "Make you glad you let me follow you home."

Bristol swallowed and lifted her face to him. "Are you finally going to kiss me?"

"Eager?"

She gave him a coy shrug. "A little."

"Let's see if we can make that a lot." He took her face in his hands.

She flashed back to the bar, in the instant before their lips had nearly met. Heart pounding, blood racing, need reeling... Yeah, she'd cursed her mother's interruption. But since then, her anticipation had grown. She wanted him more now. Maybe Mama had done her a favor in the long run. They wouldn't be interrupted here.

"You're welcome to try." She gave him a wicked grin.

He didn't say a word, just dipped his head toward her. Bristol held her breath. Her heart felt suspended in the moment and too filled with anticipation to beat. No man had ever excited her so much with a mere word or smile. She wondered how she'd handle his kiss.

"Look at me," he insisted, his voice gruff and low.

Her lashes fluttered open, and she peered up at the deepest, darkest eyes she'd ever lost herself in.

"That's it," he encouraged. "I wanted to see you, get closer to you. This may be temporary but it isn't impersonal."

"It's not," she whispered.

He caressed her face, shifted a hand behind her neck, fingers sifting through her hair. Bristol hadn't thought it possible, but he looked even more serious. "Good."

Finally, he brushed his lips over hers, the touch full of gentle command and electric thrill. A sizzle flashed over her skin. Her heart started thumping again, now beating a rapid tattoo against her chest.

Jamie pulled back enough to stare down at her again, searching her face for something. He caressed her other cheek with his warm palm. "God, I've got to taste your mouth, your skin. All of you."

Before she could say a word, he captured her lips once more, this time crashing into her, hungry, demanding, as if he couldn't get to her fast enough. He took her mouth as if he owned her, and Bristol wasn't prepared for his onslaught. His touch made her dizzy. No, *he* did. His musky scent surrounded her, dangerous, sexy, as he pressed his chest to her beating heart and consumed her.

He was above her, around her, all over her. Reaching up on her tiptoes, she threw her arms around his neck, every bit as desperate to get to him, and gasped into his kiss.

Bristol wrapped the hem of his tank in her fists and tugged up. He grabbed her wrists and swept them over her head, forcing them against the wall as he stared at her, panting, searching, naked hunger tightening his face. "Bedroom?"

The dark snap of his voice made her tremble. "End of the hall."

"Let's go." He bent and lifted her, wrapping her legs around his hips and covering her mouth with his again.

But instead of heading in that direction, Jamie shoved her to the wall and pressed himself against her. She swore she could feel his heart beating wildly. Then she forgot everything when he tightened his grip on her thighs and fitted his hips between them, rocking against her sex, right where he'd made her ache for him most.

Bristol gave a soft moan and writhed against him. It had been a while since she'd had a lover, but she had never felt anything so explosive, so connected. So right.

She pulled at his shirt again, perfectly happy with the idea that they might not make it to the bedroom. Here against this wall would be every bit as amazing, she'd bet.

He tore his mouth from hers. "How the fuck are you undoing me so fast?"

"It's…" *Chemistry.* "Something's happening between us. I…" *Need you.*

"Yeah. Me, too." He plowed her mouth again, his tongue surging deep, his kiss thorough, as if he meant to stake his claim. "I'm glad we're alone. I want to please every part of you. I want your body to know who owns it tonight. I want you to equate me with pleasure until all you have to do is hear my voice to get wet. I don't want you to have the slightest urge to ever say no."

"I can't imagine ever refusing you anything, Jamie…" She couldn't catch her breath, and it didn't matter now. Not as long as he was touching her.

He mumbled a curse before smoothing out his expression. Then he started down the hall finally, every step providing friction between them in the most delicious places. Fresh tingles erupted. Desire settled between her legs—an ache so sharp it stunned. They were still fully dressed. He hadn't done anything more than kiss her. But Bristol already suspected he would be the man by which she measured all others.

Jamie kicked the slightly ajar bedroom door open wide. Shakespurr scrambled off his perch on the windowsill with a startled meow, then scampered out of the room. Bristol barely noticed because Jamie carried her to the bed and tossed her to the mattress, following her down and covering her body with his own. He broke their kiss only long enough to tear her lacy shell from her torso and toss it across the room. Then he took her mouth again, nipping at her bottom lip and stealing inside, shredding her sanity.

Bristol tugged at his tank, frantically sliding her hands under the cotton to reach the supple skin over hard muscle. She longed to feel him, drink him in, make him a part of her for however long she could.

Finally, he tore his shirt off, sitting up enough so she could get a good look at him. Bristol nearly swallowed her tongue. Oh. Dear. God. The longer she looked at him, the more the dizzying fever of desire spun inside her. She raked her palms up the ridges of his abdomen, over the bronzed bulges of his torso. She traced the tribal tattoo on his shoulder, sucking in a breath at his iron flesh beneath her touch. Unable to resist, she skated her fingertips down his chest again, taking the time to circle one of his nipples. She delighted in watching them both go hard. Goosebumps broke out all over his body.

"Don't push me too hard, Bristol. I want to do this right." He panted, his breath coming fast as he gripped the button of his fly and tore it open. "Let me give us both a good time."

He didn't wear anything beneath his jeans. Bristol saw a shadowy hint of hair-dusted male flesh and shivered. Pressed against her earlier, he'd felt big.

"Hurry." She reached for the snap on her own jeans and tore it open, then tugged the zipper down and shoved the pants over her hips, at least until his body impeded her striptease. Quickly, he stood, shucking his own denim.

Bristol got instant confirmation about his size. Well-endowed was putting it mildly. Or maybe she'd been handling nothing but small pricks like Hayden. Literally.

"That's it, honey. Take it all off so I can get to you. I want to see that pretty skin and silky pussy before I devour them both."

No man had ever talked to her that way. His words were gritty and raw, but there was nothing dirty about them. He made her feel sexy, like a woman should.

For the first time in her life, she wanted to give a man every part of her.

She doffed her pants. Her panties followed before she reached for her bra and unhooked it. When Jamie began prowling toward her like he meant to take her in every way that would give her pleasure, her nipples peaked tight. Her sex clenched.

Heart pumping, feeling eager, she spread her legs for him, planting her heels wide on the bed. "You're too slow. Come here so I can touch you."

A hint of a smile lurked at the corners of his lips. "You're awfully bossy. Or is that impatience?"

"Would you rather debate what I'm feeling or…" She ran her fingers up the insides of her thighs, nearly brushing her own wet flesh. "Get to the good stuff?"

Jamie paused, as if debating for a moment. Then he dropped all pretense and focused his potent gaze on her. "Good stuff. In fact, let's see how good we can make it."

Before she could say a word, he covered her body, flattening her against the mattress again. Their naked chests pressed together as his face hovered over hers. The heat of his body enveloped her, warming her seemingly from the inside out. He thrust his fingers into her hair as he stared into her eyes. This might be a temporary fling—the first of her life—but somehow he managed to make her feel special with a single, searing glance.

"Kiss me," she whispered, unable to look at him without wanting more.

He dipped his head and seized her lips with his own. When he closed his eyes, he might have broken their visual connection, but his kiss gripped her heart and squeezed. He came at her as if desperate to possess her. The intensity jarred Bristol. She'd never felt like the focus of any man's desire—until now.

Then she stopped thinking altogether because he urged her lips apart with his own and plowed inside, his tongue curling against hers. Their lips mingled. Their breaths entwined. Bristol arched against him. Jamie wrapped his arms around her more tightly.

"You're so fucking sweet. And small. I don't want to break you."

She lifted her hips, rubbing against his unflagging erection. "You're big." When he laughed, she had to join him. "I meant that you're tall and all buff. It's just…when you're near I can't—"

"Not touch you?"

"Yeah," she breathed against his lips.

"I know exactly what you mean."

"This is intense."

He paused. "Very."

Relief slid through her. So he felt it, too. "I've never experienced anything like this."

Was that too honest?

Jamie glided a palm down her side, thumbing the edge of her breast, hugging the curve of her waist, before taking her hip in hand. "Truthfully, neither have I."

And he looked as if that puzzled him. Warmth oozed through her bloodstream, tugged at her heart. Shouldn't she have felt this and more with the guy she'd once hoped to marry before he'd chosen her sister? Probably, but if she wanted to keep this connection to Jamie fleeting, then she needed to stop dwelling on her feelings and start focusing on the pleasure.

She closed her eyes and kissed her way up the strong column of his neck. When he groaned, she nipped at his ear and traced her fingertips down his spine. He braced both hands on her hips and started moving, rocking his erection against her.

"Yes." She urged him on, digging her fingers into his steely shoulders.

He captured her lips again, focused and intent, as if nothing was more important than lavishing attention on her mouth with one frenzied kiss after another. Bristol drowned in his taste, let her head get dizzy with his scent. The ache between her thighs turned sharp and sweet. She had no doubt that only he could sate it.

Then he worked his way down her body, leading with his mouth, worshipping her skin as he kissed a path down her throat and over her collarbones before he zeroed in on her breasts. He paused, his hot breath exhaling over her nipples. They tightened even more. Desperation crept through her. Her ache turned urgent.

"Touch me," Bristol pleaded.

He skimmed his knuckles across one turgid peak. Sensation pinged through her body, reverberating down to her toes. She gasped.

"So perfect. So beautiful," he murmured.

Then Jamie took one hard bead in his mouth, sucking her deep. She hissed at the pull of sensation and tore off his skullcap. She'd hoped to sink her fingers into his hair and bring him closer. Instead, the dark buzz hugged his scalp and made the angular hollows of his face even more pronounced. He was all male. Another shiver of anticipation rolled through her.

He stared down at her as if he waited for something. A reaction maybe? When the moment passed in silence, he bent his head and took her other nipple in his mouth, giving this one a sweet tug, too. Then he shifted his weight onto the bed, angling himself against the side of her body so he could smooth a palm down her stomach. Bristol held her breath, her heart tripping in the seconds before he cupped her mound in his hand. He slid his fingers over her slick skin, teased at nerve endings already screaming for more. Jamie could have no doubt that she wanted him bad.

"You're wet." His voice had gone deeper, huskier.

"I'm ready," she choked out, spreading her legs for him.

Maybe she should be more modest or wait for him to make the next move, but that was the old her. The her who let herself be misled and jilted. The woman who'd emerged from those ashes demanded what she wanted without apology.

He thumbed her clit a few times, then dragged the digit through her moisture. She moaned, her mouth gaping open at the need that one mere touch sent through her body. Another few seconds and she'd probably go over the edge. *Please, yes…*

"Next time, I'm going to take you slowly and savor every bit of you. Right now, you feel so damn good. I can't wait." He bounced off the bed, then prowled to his jeans, pulling a condom free. He rolled it on virtually one-handed and frighteningly fast.

Clearly, he'd done this a lot.

Bristol felt a moment's trepidation, then stopped herself. They weren't having a relationship, merely a hookup. It didn't matter if he was a well-practiced manwhore. The only thing she should care about was pleasure.

She smiled at him. "I can't, either."

Jamie climbed back on the bed, settling his knee between her legs as he pushed her flat again. "Can you take it hard? Fast? I'm not going to be happy until you're screaming for me."

"Stop talking and start living up to your promise."

His cock jerked. Then he settled his body between her legs and gripped her hips, thrusting the head of his erection against her aching sex in one swift move. When he'd settled unerringly against her opening, he shoved forward. Hard.

His first few inches stretched her, and a sweet sting flooded her veins with drugging need. She surged up to him, her head arching back on a moan. He gripped her tighter as he eased back, then pushed deeper.

"Oh…fuck." His voice dropped lower, his raspy tone making her feel as if he was coming apart, just like her.

"More," she barely managed to squeak out.

"Yes," he growled. "Now."

Jamie delivered, withdrawing before he plunged in once more, shoving his way deeper inside her, inciting a riot of tingles. The head of his cock rubbed against her most sensitive spots. She grabbed at his shoulders, frantic to hang on as he took her close to the edge, amazed at how completely he filled her.

When he pulled back, he dragged his hard flesh over those same screaming nerves. Her heartbeat resounded in her ears. Bristol didn't care if she ever took a deep breath again. The feel of his hands on her body, of his cock working back into her would keep her more than happy.

"You're so tight. So…made for me right now. Take more." His voice deepened with dark command.

No way she could have refused him. Instead, she lifted her legs around his hips and arched closer. "Yes."

He wrapped his fingers even tighter around her hips and plunged forward again. He filled her once more, seeming to take up all the empty space inside her while relieving none of the ache. In fact, it only grew until her head swam with dizzying desire.

But he paid no heed, merely kept pressing in, squeezing another inch of his erection into her clenching flesh. He gritted his teeth, totally focused on her. Sweat dotted his temples as he shoved in yet another inch. Then a bit more.

Bristol gasped at the foreign sensation, as if he not only opened her body completely for the first time but owned it.

Finally, he tilted his hips down, fitting himself utterly against her, inside her. She writhed under him, at once frantic to end the maddening ache…yet make it last forever.

Jamie sucked in a couple of heaving breaths before he swooped down and stole into her mouth. He attacked her lips, claiming them as he withdrew his cock. She cried out in protest at his loss, but he swallowed the sound with his kiss. Then he stroked deep inside her again, stretching her to accommodate every bit of him, drowning her objection with more desire. He took down all her defenses.

He made her forget that Jamie Last-name-lacking was nothing but a fling who would be gone in a handful of days.

She didn't know how to hold anything back when he thrust into her, falling into a deep, fast rhythm that made her ancient bedframe squeak, her old floors creak, her heart thunder, and her pleasure receptors overload. Everything about him called to her, from the slightly tangy flavor of his kiss, to his scorching palms roaming her overheated skin. With every stroke, he seemed to anchor himself deeper until she would have sworn that with the feverish rise of her orgasm, he was also unzipping her skin and turning her inside out, forcing her to show every bit of the vulnerability and need she'd rather hide.

Her headboard hit the wall. Thrill zipped through her as he filled her again.

He positioned her legs up and against her body, spreading her wider, allowing him deeper. "Wrap your hands around the headboard. Don't let go."

Her heart fluttered, skipped a beat, as she complied. His triumphant smile made the ache in her sex tighten. She clamped down on him. "I'm close."

"Oh, honey. You have no idea how seriously I'm riding the edge."

Bristol didn't have a chance to say anything before he came at her again, his rhythm harder, faster, as if he'd allowed his need off a seriously tight leash. Every thrust told her that he didn't have any intention of holding back anymore.

Frantically, she grabbed at the spindles of her old brass headboard, giving Jamie what he demanded. It felt good to give in, to surrender. He rewarded her with more pleasure. Sex with him felt like embracing a thunderstorm, riding a wild bronc. She absorbed him, savoring the rising crescendo of desire as every muscle in her body tightened for the imminent explosion.

"There you are. That's it. Yeah." He gritted his teeth, staring down into her eyes, the storm there stealing her breath. "Everything about you fucking turns me on. Come for me."

She couldn't have held back for anything. Blood rushed, tingles converged, the universe parted. Angels freaking wept.

As he tensed and slammed into her again, Bristol's world crashed open, blotting out all but him. The pleasure that twisted her body wiped away everything in her head. The orgasm was too big to hold inside. She opened her mouth to beg Jamie for some way to handle the battering ram of ecstasy. The only sound that came out of her mouth was a low-pitched, animal wail.

He followed her with hammering strokes and a long, raspy growl that sounded an awful lot like her name as he shuddered.

Then he stopped, all but collapsing on his elbows above her. He planted his face in her neck, his panting breaths rolling over her skin.

He'd stolen everything from her and made her feel as if she'd been run over by a train. She didn't have the energy to even open her eyes, but she did let go of the headboard and wrap her arms around him.

"What the fuck was that?" he muttered.

"No idea." And somehow she wondered if her world would ever be the same.

Jamie lifted his head, his dark eyes shining with mischief. "Whatever it was, we definitely have to do it again."

Chapter Four

Bristol bent to bag a few cookies from the display case for Mrs. Barton's three kids and swallowed back a moan of discomfort. But putting up with the occasional twinge was a small price to pay for the enormous pleasure Jamie had given her last night.

True to his word, after that first gotta-have-it rush, he'd slowed the pace down and loved her with finessed, insatiable perfection. As their damp bodies glided together in a furious passion, he'd taken her over and over, leaving her breathless and stunned...yet still aching for him.

Clearly, he knew his way around a woman's body.

As she secured the cookies in the little white bag, Bristol sighed.

The Barton kids whooped and cheered as she handed the confections to their mom. "Thanks. Enjoy!"

After a cheerful wave, the family tumbled out into the sunshine. Once they were gone, Bristol's thoughts drifted back to the previous night. She should wipe what was probably a stupid, sappy grin from her face. But her body still hummed with a well-loved satisfaction she'd never imagined.

And when Jamie hadn't been touching her last night—which seemed constantly—he'd talked to her. About her family, her coffeehouse, her favorite movies, fondest memories...everything. He didn't talk much about himself. In fact, he'd artfully dodged most of her attempts to learn more about him. She knew some about his childhood and that, as an adult, he was a wanderer. She knew he considered his number of true friends very small. The man obviously preferred privacy. And Bristol didn't pry. As much as she enjoyed being with him, as much as he intrigued her, Jamie wouldn't be in her life past Tuesday night, provided she could even get him to stay long enough for her mother's dinner. She didn't want to find out everything about him and like him even more. She had to think fling. Temporary. Not getting attached. Romance really was nothing more than a fairy tale. Hayden and every guy she'd dated before him had proven that.

The door chime resounded overhead. And speak of the devil...

Hayden entered her shop, looking flushed. From the heat? She glanced at the clock over his head. Twenty minutes until she closed, and he knew it. When they'd been dating, he'd come by about this time when he had something on his mind. He knew it was her slowest time of day and that she couldn't end the confrontation by walking away until she locked her doors at quitting time.

Bristol tensed. "What's up?"

Hayden didn't pretend this was a friendly chat. "Is he still here?"

"Jamie?" she asked as if she had more than one man in her life. No way did she want Hayden to think she sat around pining for him. Nothing could be further from the truth.

"Yeah. I didn't appreciate you bringing him to our engagement party."

"He was my 'plus one,'" she fibbed. "I RSVPd."

"No, Jayla was your plus one," he reminded her, holding up a stern finger.

Okay, that was true but... "Why does it matter? It's not as if you ran out of food or chairs. The party wasn't negatively impacted because Jamie came."

"I didn't like it. I don't like him for you." Hayden crossed his arms over his chest.

Now that Bristol had seen Jamie do nearly the same thing—while naked—her ex seemed on the scrawny side, not deeply masculine or shiver-worthy. Seeing Hayden in the buff had never incited her to tear off her clothes and plead for his touch. But Jamie...

As she crossed the room with careful steps to straighten the bistro tables and chairs—mostly to avoid looking at Hayden—she felt that sappy smile creep across her face again. "Too bad. I do."

"That expression is making me sick. He's obviously a player. And why are you walking so funny?" He scowled, then he gaped. "Are you sore because he—"

"I won't discuss my relationship with Jamie, especially not with you,

Hayden. You're engaged to my sister now, so what I do is absolutely none of your business. Did you have a reason to come here, other than to harass me?"

He pulled down on his Sunday-best navy sport coat. "To check on you."

"I'm fine. Don't you have someplace else to be? Isn't there a church potluck this afternoon?"

"I skipped it."

Hayden never missed an opportunity to play the role of "big man in town." Bristol stared at him suspiciously. Why was he sweating? "So you could come here and bug me?"

"No." He sent her an annoyed scowl. "I stopped by Corey's house and… That doesn't matter. Watching you leave with that guy last night worried me. He won't stay, you know."

Bristol shrugged as if it didn't matter. Jamie wouldn't stay, and she was okay with that…mostly. Not seeing him after Tuesday night's dinner at her mother's house sounded horrible right now, but she was in a sex-induced infatuation bubble, right? By the time she was done with him, it was possible they both would have found a hundred ways to crawl on one another's nerves. By then, they'd realize how wrong they were together. Then she'd be ready for her next fling. No muss, no fuss. No problem.

It just didn't feel that way now.

Get it together, girl. You are not *getting your heart involved again.*

"You didn't stay either, and I survived," she pointed out.

"He's only using you for sex," Hayden added.

"I'm okay with that. At least he's putting a smile on my face. I finally understand what the big deal about sex is." She gave him a tight smile. "Shouldn't you be focusing on your sex life? After all, you and Presleigh are getting married next month."

"You know she's a virgin. We're waiting for our wedding night."

Seriously? Hayden hadn't wanted to wait ten minutes with her, and he was willing to wait over a year for her sister? *Wow.* That still didn't explain why he'd come—and why he sounded more than slightly jealous, unless…

She shoved her hands on her hips and faced him. "So you don't like Jamie here because—"

"I'm in the bed he wants to occupy until he marries his sweet little bride," Jamie called from behind her, standing in the doorway of the kitchen.

When he stepped into her restaurant, Bristol breathed a sigh of relief.

She knew he couldn't leave the building without first passing through her kitchen, and she figured he'd been sleeping after their vigorous night. But seeing him now, clearly intending to get Hayden off her back, thrilled her all over again.

Jamie skirted the display cases and headed toward her. "He's got a case of blue balls and hoped that you were pining for him enough to help him cheat on your sister so that he could dump you again when they got married. Or did you plan to just continue the bump and grind behind Presleigh's back after the wedding?"

"That is not true!" Hayden insisted. "I still care for Bristol deeply. And I'm going to make sure you don't use her and break her heart."

"You mean like you did?" Jamie prompted.

Hayden gaped like a fish out of water, the shock on his face overdone and ridiculous. "I did not. We were simply not suited—"

"We weren't, but I think you felt that way long before you bothered to share that fact with me," Bristol pointed out. "You blindsided me by telling me that you were in love with my sister. Two days later, you were dating her. Until then, you made me believe that you cared and"—she held up her hands—"You know what? It doesn't matter. I don't care if you don't like Jamie for me because *I* like him for me right now. Tomorrow may be another story, but I'm an adult. It's my life and my business. But don't for one second think you're going to waltz in here and whisper a few pickup lines, seduce me out of my clothes, and use me to pass the time until your wedding. In fact, I'd better not see or hear from you again until you say 'I do' or I'll be having a long talk with Presleigh about the likelihood of you not staying faithful."

Hayden lunged at her, his hand balled in a fist. "I wasn't hitting on you."

"Bullshit." Bristol tensed, ready to fend him off if necessary.

"And technically, I never cheated," he insisted, edging closer.

Jamie put himself squarely between them, towering over Hayden, his shoulders a formidable barrier. "I'll bet that's bullshit, too. And she *will* talk to Presleigh if you don't get the fuck out. I'll back her up."

Hayden leaned around Jamie and scowled, his expression asking her to be reasonable. She didn't see why she had to defend her decision, especially since he was acting like a jealous bully. He was the one who'd betrayed her trust. No, she couldn't prove that he'd come here today to crawl between her sheets again. But his reason certainly didn't have anything to do with concern. Was he bored? Did he need to feed his ego by wooing her into bed again? Whatever. It wasn't happening.

"Bris…" He huffed at her. "You two have known one another for…what? Ten minutes? We've known each other most of our lives. Of course I'm worried about you."

She scoffed. "I know you too well to believe that. Now go away. You know I take goodies up to the kids at the county hospital on Sundays. You're in my way."

He refused to budge.

Jamie grabbed Hayden by the shirt. "She told you how she feels. You need to respect that. Turn your ass around and leave."

"You're really going to let your boy toy talk to me that way?" Hayden demanded, shoving Jamie away. "We're practically family."

Yeah, thirty days from becoming his sister-in-law, and he wanted to nail her. No thanks. "Just go."

"I'm not leaving you here with this thug." Hayden shoved his fists on his hips and stood his ground, despite the fact that Jamie stood a good six inches above him and outweighed him by fifty pounds of muscle.

"You know, you sound tired, honey." Jamie glanced at her over his shoulder, his concern evident.

He totally ignored Hayden to check on her. Bristol tried not to let that make her a little giddy. He was merely a decent guy doing the right thing. It wasn't a romantic gesture. He might have done the same for any woman with her ex breathing down her neck.

"Three thirty this morning came early." Especially after last night. Even the thought of it made her face flush hot.

"Why don't you go upstairs and rest?" Jamie suggested.

She shook her head. "I need to lock up."

"Is it more complicated than turning the latch on the door over there." Jamie thumbed in the direction of the glass entrance.

"No. It's just…"

"Something you always do. I'll turn off the lights, too. I can handle it. Honestly."

"I have to clean up the kitchen." She glanced back at the messy space. Usually she cleaned up after herself as she cooked. This morning, she'd been too flipping tired. A night with Jamie was enough to wear out any girl, but especially one who rose at the ass crack of dawn for work.

"Go shower and eat something. It'll sit until you've rested." Jamie assured, then turned his attention back to Hayden.

Suddenly, she got it. He wanted to put her ex in his place, man to man. Bristol bit at her lip. She should tell Jamie that she could fight her own battles because she could. But the idea of a shower, a meal, and a way to avoid her ex were too much to pass up. Besides, she had the feeling he would only keep insisting.

"Sure." She smiled. "Thanks."

"Don't do this," Hayden protested. " You're making a big mistake. Talk to me."

"You let me go, so it's my mistake to make. Bye."

After a sarcastic smile and a wave, Bristol turned toward the back of the shop and headed for the stairs, feeling as if Jamie had lifted an enormous weight from her shoulders—at least for now. Come Wednesday, she'd be alone again, and Jamie would have moved on. But today, he could chase Hayden off, lock her door against the little insect, and hold her tight.

It wasn't romance, she assured herself. But it felt pretty damn good.

* * * *

Jesse heard Bristol's footfalls fade as she headed upstairs. When the door closed, he turned to Hayden with a blistering glare. "Leave her the fuck alone."

"Or what? You're not going to stay. And I'll still be around."

Hayden had him there. Jesse knew he couldn't remain indefinitely, even if sharing a bed—hell, a kiss—with Bristol was one of the most singular pleasures he'd ever experienced. For a well-seasoned hedonist, that was saying something. Still, her ex was trouble, and Jesse was determined to make sure that the asshole gave Bristol a wide berth even after he was gone.

"Are you nothing but an entitled tool who thinks you should have everything you want, and fuck everyone else?"

The scrawny guy reared back as if the question shocked him—or slapped him across the face. "What does that mean?"

"I used to be one, so I know all the earmarks," Jesse assured. "Why else would you pursue Bristol if it's only going to hurt her? You *left* her. Now she doesn't want you anymore. Obviously, that makes you feel lousy, but no one gives a shit about your pride. And young, naive Presleigh would be crushed if she had any idea you were here, sniffing around her older sister. You either care about your fiancée enough to be faithful or you're not ready for marriage."

Listen to me being all wise and shit…

"It's none of your business," Hayden shot back. "You might have spent last night with Bristol, but you don't care about her."

"And you do?" he challenged. "If you could dump her for her sister, then come back looking to get laid, I don't think you care at all."

Hayden managed to look indignant. "I came to check on her, not for sex."

"But you wouldn't turn it down, would you?"

"I-I wasn't thinking that. I…"

Hayden's seemingly perplexed expression was bullshit and told Jesse that sex with Bristol might not have been bobbing on the top of her ex's frontal lobe, but it had been swimming somewhere in his brainpan.

"The hell you weren't."

"You don't know me," Hayden finally snarled. "Fuck you."

With that, he turned and pushed out the door. The bell rang with shrill violence. The heavy glass slammed behind him.

"Good riddance," Jesse murmured, locking up and killing the lights before flipping the sign on the door to read CLOSED.

But the asshole brought up some really good points, namely that in a few days, Jesse would be gone. Right now, he didn't dig the thought of leaving Bristol behind. Kimber was the only woman he'd felt any actual emotion for in the past, and at the time he hadn't cared enough about her—or himself—to fly right. The punk he'd been years ago would probably have related to Hayden's dilemma, still being hot for one girl while engaged to another. In fact, Jesse vividly remembered the night he'd been in that position. He'd chosen wrong, siding with booze and easy ass, rather than love or respect. The decision had haunted him ever since because he knew he'd fucked up and hurt someone special. He refused to let Hayden do the same to Bristol.

While pondering ways to make the prick keep his distance, Jesse's phone buzzed in his pocket. He pulled it free and saw Candia's contact pop up on the display. A quick glance told him he was still alone in the little bakery.

He pulled up a bistro chair and answered. "Hey."

"Where are you?" She sounded frazzled.

"Did you already figure it out?" Had someone at the restaurant last night recognized him after all?

"No. You're so quiet it's eerie."

With a grin, Jesse leaned back. "Told you I wouldn't fuck it up."

"I'm actually impressed. It's a good thing you disappeared for a while."

"So things are still ugly? Why aren't the police releasing details?"

She sighed, and he heard her exhaustion. "The investigation is still ongoing. The fact that Maddy Harris died in your hotel room was bad enough. Now I've learned that she'd helped herself to the T-shirt you wore at that night's concert. She was wearing it when she died."

"Oh, shit." He could only imagine what the press were saying about that.

"Exactly. An anonymous source leaked pictures of her body at the scene. I'm betting on a cop looking to make a quick buck. Then some Photoshopping genius positioned an image of you singing that night and her lying dead in the same fucking shirt side by side. It's circulating all over social media. *ET* and *Huff Post* aren't exactly being kind in their speculation, either. But I have no doubt it's helping their numbers." She paused. "Ryan's funeral is scheduled for Tuesday morning in Shreveport. His next of kin was his great aunt. She lives there."

"I'll be there."

"Until the police conclude this investigation and some time goes by, I'm not sure you should do anything but lay low."

"I won't miss his services, Candia. If I did, I'd look like an unfeeling prick. And I need to say good-bye. He might have had his flaws, but he was my friend." He shook his head and struggled against tears. "I wish to fuck I'd been able to save him."

The rock star life looked like good-time glitz to outsiders. Living it was something else completely. Different countries, different hotel rooms, transient "friends." Jesse's schedule was never his. Indulging in his goofy side wasn't good for the badass sex-god image he'd cultivated over the years. Yeah, it sold albums, but he never quite relaxed. Music critics and a changing industry complicated everything. And the really suck-ass part was the paparazzi hovering, just waiting to snap pictures if the temptation to dive into the ever-present girls, booze, and drugs ever became too much to resist. Not for one minute did he forget that virtually everyone around him was making a buck off his vocal cords. If he lost his voice or died tomorrow, his fans would care. But would any of the people he saw day in and day out give two shits?

Not so much. Candia was the closest thing he had to a friend now, and she was a career woman first and always. If she didn't have him, she'd mourn for thirty seconds, then pick up the phone and schmooze multiple job offers before choosing one and moving on.

No wonder he'd really enjoyed his time with Bristol. She didn't expect him to be sexy or perfect or charming or anything except nice. And while he suspected she was a tad gun-shy after Hayden, she had opened up to him and shared parts of herself, like the fact that she was named after her dad's Connecticut hometown and that she watched *Buffy the Vampire Slayer* reruns whenever she caught one on TV.

"Ryan made his choices," she murmured, her voice heavy.

Jesse gritted his teeth. "When he was so high, he barely knew his own damn name."

"Sorry. I know he'd been a part of your band for years and you used to be tight." She hesitated.

Tight? They'd shared both women and parties for years. Nothing more intimate than drinking out of the same bottle while both balls deep in the same chick. He and Ryan had grown apart after Jesse had stuck with his decision to stay sober, but that didn't mean he'd cared about the guy less.

"Thanks," he muttered.

"Maddy's funeral is that afternoon in Round Rock."

He winced. What a tragic waste. Sixteen was way too young to die.

"Did you get a hold of her parents?"

"I did. They don't want anything to do with you, your apologies, or your money. And they definitely don't want you showing up to their daughter's funeral and turning it into a media circus. They want to grieve in peace. They don't blame you for what happened. Apparently, Maddy had been through some trouble with drugs in the past. But they don't want you or any token of yours around as a reminder of all they've lost. If you really want to make a gesture of some sort, I think your best option is to start a scholarship fund in her name or shoot an anti-drug PSA."

That would cost him almost nothing. Jesse wished the girl's parents had been more demanding...but forcing them to take from him would only serve to make himself feel better. "Done. Set it all up."

"Will do. Beyond that, I'm still thinking about your image and how to rehab it. Give me time." She sighed. "So where did you go after you dropped me off at the airport?"

Jesse described his road trip to see Kimber. "But I couldn't intrude on their domestic scene any longer, so I split. They won't tell anyone. Kimber understands the pressure, and Deke just wants me gone." He shifted in his seat. "After that, I went back to the hotel and grabbed my bike off the equipment truck, then took off. I pulled over to sleep at a park off the road. Then I rolled into Texarkana and found an old-school barbershop. No one in there was under seventy, so I doubt they had any idea who I am. I'd already rented a craptastic motel room and shaved. I'd taken out my earrings and slid into the jeans and a comfortable tank I keep in the saddlebag. They cut my hair without blinking. Now I'm a new man."

"So you're in Texarkana?" Candia didn't sound thrilled, and he heard her tapping on her keyboard. "Because someone there will recognize you. According to the most recent census, the city has a population of over thirty-six thousand people. Even if you've changed your appearance—"

"I was only there a few hours. I went to a nearby barbeque restaurant the barbers raved about to grab some dinner and…" Saying he'd met someone was going to launch Candia into a righteous fit. On the other hand, she seemed to have spidey senses. His publicist would figure it out, and when she realized that he hadn't clued her in, he'd have hell to pay. Besides, she couldn't help him improve his image if she didn't know how he might be impacting it. "I sort of…met a woman."

"Oh my—" she huffed. "Seriously? You think now is the time to get laid? How long before she sells you out to the tabloids? I can see the headlines now. *McCall 'grieves' with skanky one-night stand.*"

"First of all, she's not skanky and she's not a simple lay. Her name is Bristol Reese. She bakes for a living. And she's really damn sweet. Second, she has no idea who I am."

"Get real." Candia was jaded on a good day, and this wasn't a good one at all.

"I'm totally serious. She was in the middle of a weird family situation and I helped her out. She didn't recognize me. No one did. Look." He took a quick selfie of his shorn hair and clean face, bare of all leather and jewelry. Then he sent it her way. Jesse studied the image. He looked like a normal Joe.

A few moments later, he heard a ding. "Wow, that's you? Holy shit, you clean up nice. Okay, I have to admit, I barely recognize you. Your face looks leaner, more chiseled with your hair buzzed. We should talk to Jackie about making this look permanent. It's a surprisingly cool change."

Jesse didn't want to talk about his stylist now. "It's sure a shitload easier. So anyway, I'm in this small town in Arkansas. Lewisville. Barely a thousand people live here. I'm more likely to be given a sideways glance for being a newcomer than for being an international star. Relax."

She paused. "You know, maybe it's not a terrible idea for you to hang low there for a few days. I mean, if this girl has no idea who you are and you really won't see other people, that little pissant town may be the perfect place to hide."

Candia's proclamation made Jesse smile. He didn't have to give up Bristol yet. Reality would intrude soon enough, but he could enjoy her company a bit longer. He wished he could confide in her, tell her about his problems and his grief. She would listen well and give good advice, he'd bet.

"Admit it. I did the right thing," he ribbed Candia.

"In theory. It's early days. Just keep your new bug all snug in your love nest so she can't squeal. We'll talk soon."

Before he could even say good-bye, she hung up. With a shrug, Jesse pocketed his phone. In their world, time was money, and he didn't pay her to shoot the shit. He'd rather have her figuring out how to assure the public that he hadn't played any part in the girl's death and that he was sorry as hell that she was gone.

Jesse made his way back to the upstairs apartment. Not a noise disturbed the space. Shakespurr prowled closer, staring him down before he gave a disdainful meow and trotted off. But he didn't hear a sound out of Bristol.

When he crept down the hall, he found the bathroom door open, steam still clouding the mirror over the basin. A few steps more, and he stood in the door to her bedroom. She lay across the bed, dressed in a faded gray T-shirt about five sizes too big with some terrycloth turban thing wrapped around her hair. And she was fast asleep.

A fond smile crawled across his face. After her shitty evening with her family, he'd kept her awake more often than not before she'd had to slip out to work. She'd still put in almost a twelve-hour day and confronted her ex head on. His girl had smarts, stamina, and spine.

Well, she wasn't his, like, forever. But his for another day.

He'd love to wake Bristol and prove exactly how much he appreciated her, in every way he could show her. But right now, she needed sleep. If he intended to spend half the night inside her again—and he did—she'd need it. Along with some food. Then he'd have to figure out how to persuade her to let him stay for a while. He'd slip away for Ryan's service and try to avoid the press. The rest of the time, he'd spend with Bristol. That made him smile. And bonus, he would be around to fend off Hayden the half-wit. Win-win.

After pressing a light kiss to her forehead, Jesse headed downstairs again to the restaurant's kitchen. Hands on hips, he surveyed the room. It looked as if a bomb had gone off. He sighed. He was no expert with this stuff, but it couldn't be impossible to clean. It would also save poor exhausted Bristol a whole lot of effort and allow her to spend the rest of the evening with him.

As he filled the sink with soapy water and dumped all the dirty utensils inside, the events of the past few days rolled through his head.

Oddly, despite the fact that his career was in turmoil, his life upside down, and his surroundings unfamiliar, he felt completely centered. Thoughts of Bristol circled, dive-bombed. She was the reason for his Zen attitude. She amazed him. She inspired him.

A melody shot across his brain. It kind of reminded him of her—pretty, haunting, somewhat unexpected. He hummed it as he cleaned a few attachments from the standing mixer and set them out to dry. He moved onto spoons and baking pans, scouring them clean. As he wiped down the counters and display cases, Jesse realized that, despite all the crap in his life, he was smiling. Bristol did that for him. The song rolling around in his head made him kind of happy, too.

With his grin widening, he plucked his phone from his pocket and started recording the music in his head. For the first time in weeks, maybe years, he felt almost happy.

Chapter Five

Bristol awoke well after dark. She sat up with a start and found herself alone in the rumpled queen-size bed. A glance at the clock confirmed it was nearly two a.m. She'd slept ten hours. Holy cow, she never did that. Jamie had worn her out the night before, and she'd fallen into an exhausted slumber. But at least she was up early for work.

OMG, work! She'd neglected to make sure he'd locked the front door. In fact, she didn't hear any signs of him prowling around her apartment. Was he even still here?

The thought that he might have left without saying good-bye upset her way more than it should.

Scrambling out of bed, Bristol pulled on a pair of shorts and righted the towel turban on her head, vaguely wondering how bad her hair would look once she removed it. She shoved the thought aside and stumbled down the hall.

In the living room, she found Jamie. She breathed a little sigh of relief when she spotted him on her sofa with a pair of buds shoved into his ears, his phone in hand, and a notepad and pen perched on his thigh. He looked deep in thought, and she wondered what had him concentrating so intently.

When he caught sight of her, he clicked off the phone, closed the cover of the notepad, and shoved everything onto the table in a heap. "Hey, how are you feeling?"

"Kind of groggy, but otherwise all right. You hanging out? Everything okay?"

"Yeah. It's cool."

She didn't quite believe that since he gave off the vibe that she'd interrupted something. But he didn't look guilty, more like distracted. "Did Hayden give you a hard time yesterday?"

"What makes you think I'd let him?" He scoffed. "I told the little asswipe to back down. He suggested that I fuck off but I declined. It took restraint to let him walk out the door undamaged, but I let him because I didn't think mopping the floor with his face would help your situation."

Bristol didn't have much doubt that Jamie could have. "Nonviolence was probably the better choice. Sorry I crashed on you. I was beat."

He shrugged as if it was no big deal. "It's fine. You needed sleep."

Yeah, but the fact that he'd hung around waiting for her to wake up both embarrassed and excited her. Since he didn't have a job right now, it was possible he had no place else to go. Or maybe he just liked her and wanted to spend more time together. That wasn't good for her fling thing, but she'd end it soon. Any minute now… "Sorry."

"Hey, it's not a big deal. Really."

Bristol smiled when she realized he meant it. "Thanks."

"Hungry? I tossed together some stuff for sandwiches and salads last night, using your leftovers. Hope that was all right."

"Sure." She normally didn't neglect to feed her guest for over twenty-four hours. Geez, she really had been tired.

"I'll make you a plate."

She cocked her head at him. Hayden had never been half so helpful. Or caring. As soon as they'd begun dating, he'd expected her to feed him more often than not after cooking all day. He'd claimed that all his pencil pushing behind a desk exhausted him, so more often than not he'd preferred to end the day with a blow job. Less effort on his part than actual sex.

She and Jamie hadn't done more than share a bed and some skin for a few hours but already he was far more considerate. Giddy little butterflies began dancing in her belly, and Bristol had to remind herself that being a nice human being didn't mean he intended to be romantic. And they were *not* having a relationship.

"That would be great." She smiled his way.

"Give me a minute and I'll get you fed."

"Thanks. I'm going to dry my hair now and hope that I don't look like Medusa when I'm done."

"I'm pretty sure that's impossible since you're gorgeous, but go for it."

Bristol rolled her eyes at the compliment. "I look terrible. You don't have to butter me up, but I appreciate it."

As she turned for the bathroom, Jamie grabbed her wrist and snapped her around, flush against his chest. "I'm serious. I think you're beautiful. You're not calling me a liar, are you?"

His silky tone warned her that would be a bad idea. Bristol swallowed against the sudden tension in the air. "No. I just…"

"Don't take compliments well?" He raised a brow at her as if he already knew the answer. "As long as I'm around, you need to start accepting them. And believing them."

She stared up into his dark eyes in breathless disbelief. He may not be trying to romance her…but he was certainly making her heart flap and quiver. Which made her feel like a twit. She had to stop reading happily-ever-after into his nice gestures.

"Sure. Okay. Thanks." She pulled gently at her wrist, eager to leave the room before she made an idiot out of herself.

Jamie was slow to release her. "I'll have your food ready in ten. Then we can talk."

What did he want to say? She'd rather they simply had sex. She didn't find tangling between the sheets with him nearly as confusing as watching him defend her against Hayden or staring back into his eyes as he complimented her. But she had a few things to say if she was going to persuade him to go with her to dinner on Tuesday night at her mom's house, then move on afterward.

"Sounds good." She nodded his way vaguely.

After managing to brush her hair and somewhat tame the strands with a blow dryer, she tossed on her work clothes and spruced up with a dose of mascara and lip-gloss. When she tiptoed into the kitchen, she found Jamie setting a plate of what looked like a ham sandwich on thick sourdough and a mixed greens salad with some mandarin oranges and feta crumbles.

She sat and blinked down at her plate. "You did this?"

"Yeah." He shrugged. "My parents worked a lot when I was a kid. I learned how to fend for myself by foraging from the fridge. This is easy. It's not as difficult as making turducken. Or your fabulous cookies."

But she really couldn't think of the last time anyone had cooked for her. It was a small gesture. Maybe this was his way of thanking her for letting him crash here. But that intent gleam from his dark eyes sparkled with something far more personal than gratitude.

Her breath caught. Her heart loped into a gallop. "I'm sure it's great.

I really appreciate it. And I'm, um…glad you didn't bail while I slept."

"About that…" For the first time since she'd met him, Jamie looked uncomfortable. "Look, if you don't need me to go, I'd love to stay a few days."

Did he need money? Was he between jobs or houses? Did it really matter since he only wanted a few days and she needed him to stick around that long? No, but everything felt more complicated because some silly part of her didn't want to let him go.

Bristol studied him. "You okay?"

He pulled at the back of his neck. "Yeah. I'd like to spend some time with you before I go back to work."

"So you do have a job?"

Jamie laughed. "Yeah. I'm…taking a vacation right now. I haven't had one in years."

"And you travel a lot. What do you do?"

"No offense, but one reason I'm taking this vacation is so that I don't have to talk or even think about work for a while. You understand, right?"

As someone self-employed, she understood the constant pressure, the stress of being unable to simply have a few days off. If someone had given her that golden opportunity, she probably wouldn't want to talk about her job, either. Besides, unless she was going to move him into the "relationship" category, she didn't need to know everything about him. "Sure. Totally understand."

"Thanks. I want to use this time to be with you because I…like you. A lot. That probably sounds corny. It's been rough lately but being with you is peaceful. Nice." He shook his head. "I'm saying it wrong. I feel good when I'm with you."

That insidious butterfly took up residence in her tummy again, but Bristol couldn't seem to squash him. She felt a bit like the cute guy in school had told her that he wanted to "go" with her.

Wiping the smile off her face proved impossible. "You made me feel pretty good last night, too."

He grinned. "We were damn hot together. But even hanging with you is great. We…click."

"I should disagree. After all, we're just hooking up." But she felt a school-girly grin cross her face again. "But we do click. So if you're going to stay, would you come with me to my mom's house for dinner on Tuesday night?" She winced. "She told everyone you would be there."

"And you don't want to brave it alone?"

"Not really. Please…" She sounded as if she was wheedling because she was.

"Well, I don't want to leave you alone with the wolves. Will Presleigh and Hayden be there?"

"Yep, along with half the town. I'd really appreciate it. As Jayla put it, if I come alone I'll look like a ho-bag who's not interested in keeping a man." Bristol realized that made her sound as if she might be looking for some commitment. "And I'm not interested in hanging onto anyone after my shit with Hayden, but I'm really not eager to be the center of town gossip, either."

A frown wrinkled Jamie's brow before he bent and pressed a lingering kiss on her lips. Affection with a teasing hint of passion. One touch, and Jamie made her ache for more.

He eased back, staring down into her face. "I'll go with you. Now eat. I'm going to grab a shower, if that's cool."

Bristol let out a sigh of relief. "Yeah, help yourself. And if you want to wash some clothes, I've got stackable units in the closet in the hallway."

"I appreciate it." Jamie nodded, heading for the bathroom.

She grabbed a coffee, devoured her meal, then found her shoes shoved half under the bed. Downstairs, she began flipping on lights, grabbing ingredients as she made her way from the stockroom toward the kitchen, not looking forward to the cleanup she'd neglected yesterday. It would tack on an extra hour to her day, but she'd obviously needed the sleep last night. Now it was time to pay for the indulgence.

But when she entered the kitchen, nothing but clean dishes and sparkling surfaces awaited her. Her jaw dropped. Someone had cleaned everything, set up her mixer again, put away her utensils, even mopped the usually sticky floor.

Someone? The only person who could have done that was Jamie.

Her heart stuttered then skipped. Bristol might wish she could find a way to not care about Jamie…but that wasn't happening now. Why fight what was so damn obvious? She was falling for him.

Jamie looked after her and helped her out. She enjoyed his banter. The sex was so far beyond mere pleasure that she didn't have the words to describe it. Their "click" was undeniable. She'd shared much less with Hayden and considered the idea that maybe he was "the one," at least until he'd dumped her for her sister. But Jamie was so much…more.

Was it even possible for her to stop her feelings for him from growing?

Bristol pushed the question aside, at least for now. She glanced at her phone. She still had about forty-five minutes before she had to be back in the kitchen to ensure the dough for her cinnamon rolls rose properly before baking them for opening.

Shoving the phone back in her pocket, she charged up the stairs again and found Jamie coming out of the bathroom with a towel wrapped around his lean waist. Water droplets dotted his hard flesh, rolled in the ridges between his chest, and down his abdomen. A sting of need flared between her legs. She swallowed hard, then ran at him.

Jamie caught her as she wrapped her arms and legs around his waist and covered his lips with her own. He didn't hesitate, simply plunged into her mouth with a moan and cupped her ass in his hands, as he eased them back toward her bedroom. Suddenly, she felt the mattress at her back and his body covering hers.

He lifted his head, searching her face. "To what do I owe this pleasure?"

"Thank you. Thank you. Thank you."

"You're welcome. What did I do?" He grinned. "Because if you're going to thank me this way for a sandwich and a salad, I'll feed you all day long."

She found herself honest-to-goodness giggling. "I appreciate that, too. I meant cleaning my kitchen downstairs."

Jamie brushed her hair back from her face. "So the fact that I cleaned your utensils all spick-and-span makes your ovaries flutter?"

"That makes me sound easy." She grimaced.

He shook his head. "That makes you sound adorable. You're not like other women."

"We covered this once. I know, I don't get all gussied up and pray properly to the Revlon gods."

"Screw that. I mean, you don't try to be anyone except yourself. You don't act differently to please your mother. You didn't put on a face to impress me. And you certainly had no problem telling Hayden how you feel."

Bristol cocked her head. "I guess some people don't act like themselves when others are watching. That baffles me. Seems like a lot of effort merely to be miserable."

He nodded slowly. "Let's just say I've met a lot of unhappy people over the years. Neurotic, insecure, self-absorbed. Hell, I was one for a long time. I didn't really feel like myself for a decade."

"I can't picture that." He seemed so natural, so normal. "And where are you meeting these awful people?"

"They're everywhere. I can't tell you how thrilled I am to be with someone so real."

He cut off the conversation by kissing her again, devouring her as if he was hungry, as if they hadn't touched in a decade.

Then she stopped thinking entirely when he peeled off her clothes and lost his towel. He tossed everything to the floor and grabbed a condom from his nearby jeans.

After making her scream a couple of times so loudly she wondered if everyone on her block could hear, Bristol draped herself over his steely chest, still damp from exertion, and pressed a kiss between his pectorals. At the moment, she felt too sated to do anything else.

"I'm happy, too. You're a really decent guy," she murmured, looking up his hard torso, into those dark eyes that had the power to make her shiver. "You're considerate and helpful, not the sort of douche who would deceive me, like Hayden."

He smoothed his big hand over her crown and smiled. "Are you saying you like me, too?"

"Yeah," she admitted. *Way more than I should.* That realization made her a little uncomfortable because she worried it would end up one-sided, so she slid out of bed and grabbed for her clothes. "Um…I should get to work. I'm running late."

With a promise to drop in downstairs once he woke, Jamie gave her a lingering kiss good-bye. Bristol tried not to feel that jittery, excited, falling-in-love thing. But she failed miserably because it coursed through her veins and squeezed her heart as she tiptoed down the stairs. She was so deliciously sated that she didn't care she was twenty minutes late getting back to her kitchen. Nope. She simply headed for her dough, pushing thoughts of tomorrow aside and wearing a big ol' smile on her face.

* * * *

In a ridiculously good mood, Bristol turned on the radio and swayed to the music while she made goodies for her patrons that day. The bounce in her step was probably leftover pleasure hormones drifting through her body and the happiness of knowing that she'd get to be with Jamie for another few days.

After a few crying-in-her-beer songs, Bristol changed the station from her usual contemporary country music to the happier Top-40 station out of Texarkana. She didn't recognize many of the songs and artists since this wasn't her usual thing, but this music matched her mood.

The hours slid by, and she figured Jamie would be sleeping. When she baked her first pan of cinnamon rolls, she took two upstairs and left them on the counter for him with a note. As she turned, she skirted the coffee table, heading for the door. One glance at the glass slab topping the pair of whiskey barrels proved that the notebook in which Jamie had been writing earlier was gone, but he'd left his phone behind. Bristol hesitated.

She couldn't deny a gnawing curiosity to know more about him. But peeking at his phone would be prying. Even if she blew past her principles, she would either be wildly disappointed or even more intrigued, depending on what she found. Nope. So they'd crossed into temporary friends-with-benefits territory. Maybe even a bit more. Still, that didn't mean she needed to know his deepest thoughts. Because no matter how she defined their relationship, that didn't entitle her to invade Jamie's privacy.

With a sharp nod, she left the phone untouched and made her way down the hall to find him sprawled out in her bed, one bulging arm thrown over his head, the bronzed ridges of his chest and abs bare. She cursed the sheet riding low on his hips, covering everything else.

At a glance, he looked like the dangerous sort of man, built of brawn and brute strength. If he'd lived in another time, Jamie could have slayed his enemies with a quick slice of his sword before he claimed his woman with a ferocious kiss. God, she really had to stop the over romanticizing, even if she did have an amazing man in her bed.

When he sighed in his sleep, Bristol couldn't help the fond smile that crept over her face. He was more than gorgeous. He had a kind side. And he liked her. Having him here felt comfortable. Right. And it wasn't simply because she didn't want to be alone and he would do. Hayden had been here many times, and she'd always been a bit relieved when he'd left. No, around Jamie she simply felt grounded, like life was as it should be.

Dangerous thoughts.

Shaking her head, she headed back downstairs. The buzzing alarm on her phone reminded her when it was time to open the shop, so she started her first pot of coffee and waited for old Mr. Jones, who was eighty if he was a day. But he came every morning like clockwork at six thirty.

Sure enough, as soon as she unlocked the door, he ambled in. Sun began streaming through her windows. He took a seat and she set a mug of coffee in front of him, along with a bowl of sugar and a cinnamon roll, as always. She watched him doctor his coffee with somewhere north of a half dozen teaspoons of sugar.

"You know too much sugar is bad for you." She grinned. Every day, they gave one another a hard time about something. She usually let him win.

He waved her away, his old black hand gnarled with arthritis now. "When you're my age, you feel like you've defied death for years. Bring it on, I say."

Bristol laughed. "Well, if I had your metabolism and didn't have to worry about the size of my hips, I'd probably say the same thing."

"You're a pretty thing. When is some smart man going to scoop you up?"

"Maybe marriage isn't for me." She shrugged. "I mean, I already struggle to do my own laundry. The thought of doing someone else's is awful."

"I married Mildred because my mama told me it was time to look after myself and I didn't know the first thing about cooking."

That wasn't entirely true, but Bristol let him talk. "Well, I know she fed you since you made it all these years."

"Yeah, but not a day has gone by since I lost my wife that I haven't wished I'd married her sooner so I could have spent more time with her. God rest her soul."

Bristol's heart fluttered. Mr. Jones's longing made her wistful for something more. Her time with Jamie had probably contributed to that, too. She really had to stop romanticizing the man. One more nice gesture on his part and she'd probably fall head over heels. Once he figured it out, he'd likely wonder what the hell was wrong with her.

"I know she would say the same if she could be with us," Bristol said softly and took his hand.

The old man closed his eyes and gave her a squeeze. "Find your someone while you're young enough to build a whole lot of years together and share the love. Houses and jobs come and go. But there's nothing better than having someone who's your home."

She gave him a smile, trying not to tear up and show him her sadness. But every word he'd said called to her heart's deepest desire. Her grandmother had once told her that she was meant to be married. But instead of baking for her husband and kids, she did so for the townsfolk. She mothered a cat. More often than not, she spent her intimate time with a vibrator.

Bristol wanted more. The insidious thought crept in that she wanted Jamie.

Nodding at the old man, she gave his hand one last squeeze before she turned away, taking an unnecessary trek to wipe off the counter next to the display case. It gave her a good reason to bow her head and collect herself.

"I would, but none of the guys of my generation are as handsome or as fabulous as you."

"You'll find someone. You're too sweet to be alone." He grinned. "And some smart fella who can't cook for himself is going to treasure you."

"From your lips to God's ears." She winked as he rose slowly from his chair, left some money on the table, grabbed his cane, and made his way out the door.

Mr. Jones had given her food for thought. She wasn't that woman who couldn't be complete without a man. She didn't hate the life she'd built for herself. She wasn't old-fashioned, and she certainly had aspirations of her own. But Bristol couldn't deny she'd like to be a wife and mother.

Someday.

With a sigh, she headed back into the kitchen and worked her way through the majority of the morning customers. One of the new schoolteachers came in for a dozen cookies for her hardworking students as the end of the school year approached. A few stay-at-home moms popped in for coffee and veggie omelets on their way to yoga. The guys from the drugstore down the street came to snag an assortment of goodies for their post-lunch treat. When she looked up again, it was nearly eleven a.m. She'd have another lull before her few lunch customers came in, so she hustled to toss together a few salads and sandwiches for the display case.

The radio still hummed in the background, now playing a new song of Jesse McCall's. She grinned when she remembered the crush she'd had on him in high school. The new song was infectious and a little biting, with a hint of sexy, but she liked it. When it ended, the deejay took over the airwaves.

"Scandal has been good for McCall's new album. It's number one in its second week. An official statement says he deeply regrets the overdose of a fan and the suicide of his bandmate. His publicist says he's taking some time off to grieve, but a source close to the singer says no one has seen or heard from him in days. One of our listeners e-mailed this morning to say they think they saw him recently at Bubba Oink's Bone Yard, cozying up to a brunette. Anyone else spot him?" The deejay laughed. "While y'all speculate on that, I've got another tune coming your way from Bruno Mars."

Presleigh and Hayden's engagement party had been at Bubba Oink's. Bristol would have liked to spot Jesse McCall there, to see if he was as hot in person as he was in pictures. During high school, she'd had a notebook with him on the front, and she'd loved staring into his dark eyes during geometry and fantasizing…

She put the brakes on that thought. Dark eyes. Bubba Oink's. A man without a last name who was taking a little time off from work and didn't want to talk about his past…

No, that man in her bed could *not* be Jesse McCall. They didn't look that much alike, did they? That thought must be her overactive imagination stretching. Still, she withdrew her phone and launched her browser, bringing up images of the singer. None of them showed him with short hair or a skullcap or a clean-shaven face. But now that she looked closely, the shape of the face seemed similar. In most images he wore earrings, sometimes more than one. Jamie didn't sport any, but she'd noticed three empty holes in each ear. His eyes looked like a dead ringer for the rock star's.

Bristol scrolled a bit more, then came to an image that made her blood freeze in shock. Jesse McCall shirtless, with the same tribal tattoo on the same shoulder that she'd traced with her fingers, her tongue.

It was possible Jamie had gotten the ink to look like Jesse.

Or maybe Jesse McCall was hiding out in her apartment from the rest of the world and whiling away his time by having sex with her until his most recent media storm died down.

It seemed crazy, almost impossible. Almost…but not quite. Either way, she needed the truth.

Trying not to shake, she brought up Jayla's contact on her phone and called.

"Hey, girl!" her friend answered.

"Can you come over here and mind the restaurant for a bit? Everything is made. All you have to do is work a cash register." Bristol's voice shook with anger. If what she suspected was true, then he'd deceived her. He'd preyed on a woman who'd recently recovered from another asshole, using her without a care for how she'd feel.

"Is something wrong?"

"Maybe. I need…" Bristol didn't want to explain now. She didn't want to do anything but get to the truth. "Can you?"

"Sure thing. I'll be there in fifteen. What are you going to do?"

"I might be giving our friend Jamie a huge piece of my mind."

Chapter Six

The sound of a slamming door woke Jesse. He sat up in bed, disoriented. Immediately, he knew he wasn't in a hotel room—thank god—but in Bristol's bedroom. The whole place smelled like her, something that teased his senses with cinnamon and woman. He glanced at the clock and frowned. Had she come back for lunch?

He heard footsteps marching down the hall, coming at him rapidly. That didn't sound like the gait of a happy woman.

Jesse swung his feet over the side of the bed and shoved on his pants. He was buttoning them when he caught sight of Bristol as she reached the doorway, looking tense and barely shy of furious.

"What's wrong, honey?" A nasty suspicion took root in his head. "Did Hayden come back? Because if he did, I'll—"

"What's your last name?"

The out-of-nowhere question made Jesse freeze. Was she onto him? "Does it matter?"

"You know it does."

So she'd figured him out. And she was pissed. Most of the women he'd known in his adult life would be thrilled to learn his identity. They'd be ecstatic to realize they'd been screwing a star. Not Bristol.

On soft footfalls, he headed in her direction. "Let's sit down and talk about this."

"I don't want to sit down." She gritted her teeth. "I want an answer. Did you or did you not lie to me about who you are?"

He rubbed at his forehead. He would have liked to brush his teeth and have some coffee before this confrontation. That would buy him some time so he could figure out what to say. The usual charm with his rock star smile and a flash of dimples wasn't going to cut it. He wanted her to understand that he'd never meant to hurt her. He couldn't let her think for an instant that he'd used her or didn't give a shit.

Because as far as he could tell, Bristol was the first woman he'd cared about in a long fucking time.

He took her shoulders in a light grip, his head racing. "I'm sorry."

She shook him off. "Maybe after we'd shared the sheets a time or two, you might have bothered to mention that I'm not sleeping with Jamie No-last-name, but Jesse freaking McCall. Were you ever going to tell me?"

Her eyes filled with tears, and the guilt gouged his heart.

"You kept hinting that we were merely hooking up." He shrugged. "At first, that was fine. I thought you were interesting and I needed a place to lay low. You've heard about my bandmate and the awful tragedy last week?" When she nodded, he reached for her again. "I wasn't there. I had nothing to do with it. My publicist told me to go underground while she worked on communicating that to the public. It made sense." He tried to smile. "Besides, she's scary. I tend to do what she says."

The quip fell flat. Hurt crossed her face. "So I was a way to pass the time while you hid from everyone? Great."

"No." He got serious again. "It would have been better for me if I didn't care about you so damn much, but from the beginning something about you grabbed onto me and wouldn't let go. It's why I jumped in to help you back at that barbeque dive. I couldn't look at your sad eyes and not want to make you happy. I still can't."

"So you feel sorry for me? Gave me a few pity fucks?"

"God, no! I like you. Remember?" Jesse more than suspected his feelings for Bristol went deeper, but he wasn't sure she would hear him now—or believe him. "But being famous, I have to be careful. People have sold me out before. Folks I've hired or I thought were my friends have taken pictures of me or prowled through my personal information and sold it. You've seen the pictures of me in the shower?"

She nodded sheepishly. "Everyone has. Didn't some girlfriend of yours take them?"

"Supposedly. Five weeks into the relationship, she chose half a million dollars over me. So you're not the only one who's felt used."

"That's terrible. I would never…" She shook her head.

No, she wouldn't violate his privacy like that. He might not have known her as long as he had Sierra before she'd betrayed him. Bristol wasn't a fame monger. She knew what being used felt like.

"I get that now," he assured. "At first, I wasn't sure, and what I did know of you... I really wasn't sure whether you wanted revenge sex so you'd have something to shove in Hayden's face or if you actually liked me."

Her expression softened for a moment, and Jesse hoped that meant he was reaching her. "I do like you." Then she toughened up again. " Or I did. If you thought I was only using you, why did you come home with me?"

"Honestly? I wanted you too much to pass you up. I meet a lot of women..."

That full mouth of hers pinched and she crossed her arms over her chest. "Of course you do. You'd said that. Now I understand."

And Bristol's expression said that she felt stupid. When she closed her eyes as if castigating herself, Jesse couldn't stand there and not touch her.

He closed the distance between them and crushed her against his body. When she struggled to break free, he held her tighter and set his lips against her ear. "Please let me hold you. What I'm trying to say is that I knew you were different immediately, and I liked you so much that I couldn't walk way. I've spent a decade with people who didn't mean anything to me. You're different. But I had to know you before I could risk telling you who I am."

She didn't say a word for the longest time, merely crossed her arms over her chest as if protecting herself. But he could see the wheels turning in her head, examining the situation. He thanked god she was too polite not to listen and too logical for his rationale to escape her.

"I hear what you're saying," she said finally. "In your shoes, I probably wouldn't have told me, either. I shouldn't be upset that you had to protect yourself from a near stranger because you didn't know if I would sell you out. But that doesn't make being lied to hurt less."

Jesse felt guilty for not believing in her sooner and coming clean, but grateful she understood, at least on some level. "Hurting you was never my intention, so I really am sorry for that. But I think you also never expected to care about me." He curled a finger under her chin but she resisted meeting his gaze. "Are you this upset because you do?"

Her eyes widened to big green pools of confusion and contrition. More tears shimmered, threatening to spill. "I swore off relationships. I'm bad with romance."

"*You're* bad...or you've tried it with the wrong people? I've made the same mistake." He took a deep breath, diving head first into the already deep conversation. "I'm going to put the truth out there. I've never felt this way with any other woman."

Instantly, she shot him a scathing, skeptical stare. "You don't have to let me down easy with a lie."

"I wouldn't bother." He anchored his hands in her hair and clenched his fists. "If you were anyone else, after the sex I would have already shrugged and walked away."

"So you're saying all those celebrities and groupies you've screwed don't hold a candle to me? Right..."

Her sarcasm bit, and he tugged on her hair. "They didn't. Everything about you makes sense to me. And let me tell you, nothing in my life has made sense in a long time—especially not relationships. You're pretty without artifice, kind even to the people who have wronged you, smart, ambitious. And you're refreshingly not narcissistic or mercenary. You admitted that we click."

Agreement crossed Bristol's face, though she didn't say it aloud. "So?"

"I'm going to ask again, are you this upset because you didn't want to care about me? Or because it shocks you that you do?"

She pulled away from him with a huff, her little fists clenching. "Why can't I be normal? The rest of the free world can find someone and hook up for a day or two without getting involved emotionally. The first time I try, what happens? Yeah, I wind up being all giddy and excited. You walk in the room and I feel something in my stomach flutter. I can barely wait to touch you. Or even talk to you. I have to remind myself not to fall in love. And now I'm making an idiot out of myself with one of the most famous people on the planet." She shook her head. "I was already aiming high with the prince of Lafayette County because he was nice to me once upon a time and—"

"Don't beat yourself up about Hayden. He's the deficient one. He broke apart from you to be with your sister because he can't equal you in intellect, ambition, or character. He found someone more his speed. If he'd stayed much longer, you would have realized he wasn't for you."

She shrugged. "Maybe."

"He left you before you could beat him to it. He probably felt outdone by you. But don't for one second think that small-town prick split because you weren't good enough for him, so therefore you're nowhere near enough for me. It's bullshit, and I'll argue with you all day long."

"Hayden doesn't matter anymore."

"He doesn't, but we do. And I'm sorry I wasn't on the up-and-up, but you know why. I'm not letting you go over this crap." He shrugged as if his mind were made up. "I'm seriously not."

She took a shuddering breath, tears still threatening to spill. "How did I come in to confront you about lying to me and wind up feeling like the dysfunctional head case?"

He laughed. If Bristol could tell even a sideswiping sort of joke, then he must have said something that reached her. "Well, I usually feel like a dysfunctional head case and I didn't want to be alone."

She gave him a watery grin. "You suck."

"Not yet, but if you lose the clothes, I'll be happy to find some part of you I can get my mouth on."

With a playful swat on the shoulder, she sniffled. "I'm sorry."

"Don't be. I know exactly why you were upset. No one likes to be lied to. Honestly, it's a relief to me that you know the truth. And now you can stop calling me Jamie. Every time you cry out that name during sex, I want to punch my cousin."

"Is that his name?" When he nodded, she giggled. "No wonder you grimaced a lot."

"Next time, I want to hear *my* name on your lips. And don't say there won't be one."

"I want there to be one, too." She took a deep breath. "But you've got a lot on your plate and a career to go back to. My life is here. And really, where could we take this?"

Damn, she was fighting the relationship thing hard. She had no idea how willing he was to fight back. "I don't know but I'm not giving up merely because it doesn't look obvious or it won't be easy. We're going to take it one day at a time, okay?" At her uncertain stare, he tried to bite back his frustration. "What's making you hesitate most. The fame? My crazy past? The newness of our relationship?"

She shook her head. "All of it."

Her hesitation was understandable. That didn't make him less impatient to be done with it. "First, you may not think you know me well, but I will never fuck you over like Hayden. I already know you're not the kind of girl to sleep with a celebrity simply because you can or want to get pregnant for a payday. The getting-to-know-you thing will take time. So will total trust. But I'm willing to be all in if you are."

"Just like that?"

"Yeah. Because I've tried everything else, so I know something good when I find it. The fame is fleeting and not real. I mean, yes, I have paparazzi chasing me and a monster social media presence. I've got screaming fans who don't always know how to observe proper boundaries. But this also allows me to make a hell of a nice living and to do some good in the world through various charities. I try not to take it too seriously, especially since it could all be gone tomorrow."

She gave him a shaky nod. "And the rest?"

"I can't undo my past. There was a lot of booze and drugs. I did a bunch of crazy, off-the-chain shit. Because at seventeen, nothing sounds more awesome than living the ultimate rock star fantasy." He shook his head at the waste of it all. "It took me a decade but I finally started questioning whether I *should* do any of that wild crap. So I sobered up, and that part of my life is done. Sobriety has given me a clarity about life I've never had. Losing Ryan has made me realize that life can be even more fleeting than I thought."

"I'm sorry for your loss," she murmured, reaching for his hands and giving them a squeeze.

Jesse clutched at her. "He was a friend. When I changed my ways, it pissed him off. We used to get wasted and tag team women together. I won't lie; we did it a lot. Once I decided to change, he had no one to party with. He started using more, fucking random girls more. I couldn't reach him. I couldn't stop him."

When he choked back his guilt, Bristol slid closer to him. "It's not your fault."

"No, he made his choices. Just like I made mine. But I'll always wonder if I could have said or done something different to help him. If I could have saved him."

"Don't feel guilty for surviving. You did what you had to do for you."

He nodded. "I knew if I didn't, I was going to die. The morning I woke up on a hotel balcony puking next to Ryan, five naked girls passed out around us, hung over like a bitch with no idea what continent I was even on, I knew something had to change."

Bristol withdrew her hands. "That's a lot of women."

"Yep. More than I even remember." He shrugged. "But I can honestly tell you that I've never stood in front of any of them and truly tried to work out our relationship. I was engaged once to a friend years ago. She ended up marrying another guy and they're expecting baby number two. That's the most serious relationship I've had. Until you."

"I've slept with three men in my life, including you. And obviously you've been with hundreds of girls."

Probably more. "The number doesn't matter. None of this is about genitals. It's about feelings. I have them for you. I think you have them for me."

For a long moment, Bristol looked afraid to be honest. Finally, she nodded. "Yeah."

"So we're beyond a hookup. It's up to us to figure out where to go from here. Who's watching the restaurant?"

"Jayla."

"So…you don't have to be downstairs again right away?" He sent her a smile rife with seduction.

Bristol hesitated, then pulled her phone from her pocket and dashed off a text. A ding came moments later. Then she met his stare with a challenge of her own. "Jayla says all is quiet for now, so I could probably stay another minute or two."

He prowled closer, unbuttoning his pants and lowering his zipper. "How about an hour or two?"

She stood her ground, her gaze dipping down to where he peeled away his jeans. "I don't know if I've forgiven you yet."

"I'm willing to do whatever it takes to make sure you do," Jesse murmured across her cheek as he grabbed the hem of her T-shirt and shoved it up. Before he'd whisked it over her head, he'd worked the clasp of her bra open, then peeled them both off at once. The second the garments cleared her body, he covered her lips with his own and sank inside her velvety mouth, stealing inside to claim her.

They'd spoken a lot of words to one another. She'd heard him…for the most part. But now he wanted them to communicate in a way he felt certain she'd understand completely.

"Shoes off," he insisted.

Then he set to work at the fastenings of her pants while drowning in the taste of her kiss. As he slid them down her hips, she kicked her tennis shoes aside and wriggled her hips until the denim fell to her ankles and she stood before him in nothing but a tiny pair of white lace panties.

Jesse smiled as he released the messy pile of her brown hair shimmering atop her head. As the waves cascaded around her shoulders, heat settled in his belly. Blood rushed to his cock. Yeah, this woman did it for him, excited him in ways he hadn't known a woman could. For the first time in his life, he wanted to be a better person—enough to do the hard work to improve himself, not use her for some quick fix to normalcy and improved self-esteem, the way he'd tried with Kimber years ago. He intended to be a better man for Bristol. He intended to keep her beside him, wake up every morning to her smile.

Heavy realizations. But Jesse couldn't remember a time he'd felt clearer or more certain.

"Now lose the underwear," he demanded. "Slide them down your hips slowly and let me see what I'm craving."

She cocked her head. "What if I don't take orders from you?"

Oh, now she was challenging him. He just smiled. "I can take what I want."

"I dare you," she breathed.

He understood what she was playing at. If she gave in too easily now, it would bend her pride. Instead, she challenged him to take her body and push the issue of her surrender.

Game on.

Jesse anchored his hands around the fragile undergarment at her hip and pulled. The seam unraveled for him—precisely like he intended she would under his touch.

When she stood naked before him, she shivered. He watched the shallow rise and fall of her breast, the movement of her hard nipples as the midday sun slanted through her window. Her fair skin looked luminous and golden. No spray tan for her. No chemicals that made her reek or look like an Oompa Loompa. Bristol was classic and alabaster, appearing untouchable.

But he definitely intended to touch her—and more. She wasn't leaving this bed until she knew she belonged with him.

Jesse bent and lifted her against his body, following her down to the mattress. He didn't give her an opportunity to wriggle away, simply anchored his hips between her thighs and pinned her down. She felt so small beneath him, and he braced an elbow near her head to take some of his weight off her.

She met his stare. Those leafy green eyes of hers were a sight he'd never get tired of.

"Jesse," she whispered.

The uncertainty on her face broke his heart. "Close your eyes. Yeah," he commended as she did. "Take a deep breath. That's it." He bent to whisper in her ear. "Any doubts you have we'll talk out later. Right now, I want to worship you."

Bristol gave a low moan. Against him, she trembled. Then so slowly it made him sweat, she opened her eyes, her arms, and finally her heart to him. Given his past, he probably didn't deserve her, but he intended to do everything possible to make her glad she'd chosen him.

She clung to his shoulders, and Jesse brushed the hair from her face and worked his lips up her neck. "Feel how good we are together."

With a little shiver, she nodded. He fanned a hand over her breast, his thumb brushing her taut nipple. She arched into his touch and thrashed under him. He swallowed the sound with his kiss, aligning their bodies until he was flush against her, not merely covering but enveloping her. Jesse wanted to take all of her, make sure she knew that she was his. A sizzle shot up his spine when he thought about the pleasure of making love to her. But more than anything, he simply ached to feel her close.

Yeah, he had it bad. Never in a million years had he thought he would fall hard and fast for a down-to-earth baker. On paper, she wasn't his usual—not loud or flashy or sexually aggressive. Yet everything about her shy sparkplug of a personality fascinated him. Almost from the first, he'd felt as if some invisible wire attached them, tugging him closer and closer to Bristol. Until her, he hadn't really known that sort of pull was possible.

Jesse positioned her arms above her head, splayed on the mattress, then eased his hands up her silky flesh from elbows to palms, finally curling his fingers around her wrists. He anchored her to the bed and buried his nose in the cinnamon musk of her neck, closing his eyes as the light brown silk of her hair caressed his shoulder and teased his senses.

Beneath him, she softened, a gasp escaping her throat as she tossed her head back, as if the pleasure somehow surprised her. Jesse took the opportunity to drag his lips up her oh-so-soft skin before working his way to her mouth and dominating the sweet bow with a slanting, possessive kiss.

Endless. Timeless. The joining of their mouths went on. All the things that made Bristol unique piled on top of his senses.

She responded without artifice, exactly as she had the first time he'd taken her to bed. Her glimmering green eyes stared up at him, soft with raw emotion, as he skated one palm down the lush under curve of her pert breasts, her small waist, the feminine flare of her hips. True, she had the same basic parts and curves as every other woman he'd fucked, but she alone made him feel this electric gravity when they touched. When he was near her, his head buzzed, his dick engorged, and his heart chugged.

Jesse didn't see how he could possibly give her up.

Needing to inhale more of her, he made his way down her body, claiming the sweet expanse of her skin as he descended past her delicate collarbones, the swells of her breasts, her tight nipples begging for his tongue. He took them all, gliding his lips over the sensitive flesh before teasing with his tongue, nipping with his teeth.

Beneath him, she wriggled and moaned in arousal. The sweet music filled his ears. The melody he'd been writing for her played in his head, and the bridge that had stumped him last night suddenly rolled across his imagination. It sounded like a more sensual rhythm than he'd been chasing yet so perfect. So her.

The notes played a soundtrack in his head as he dipped down again to nibble at her hipbones and drag his lips over the slight curve of her belly. Jesse even liked that she wasn't perfect and didn't have the sort of personal training regime that made him feel as if he was cozying up to a bodybuilder rather than a woman.

"Spread your legs," he murmured as he caressed her mound, using his thumbs to open her folds for him.

Bristol's breath hitched. She hesitated before slowly revealing everything he desired to his ravenous stare.

Jesse hissed. She was already wet and swollen. He glanced up her body, into her eyes. They were glassy and unfocused. Her cheeks looked flushed. The sight of her arousal slammed him in the chest. He'd fucked politician's daughters and porn stars. But he'd never been with a woman he wanted to please this badly.

He dragged his fingers through her wet flesh, focusing on the little bud hardening more with every circle of his practiced fingers. "You're pretty."

After breathing in her velvet scent, he dragged his tongue through the wet groove of her sex, lingering exactly where she would be sensitive, igniting nerve endings he knew would drive her wild.

Beneath him, she thrashed, swinging her head from side to side. He knew she wasn't negating the pleasure as much as she was trying to assimilate it. He often felt the same way as soon as she put her hands on him.

"You're sweet," he muttered in between strokes of his reverent tongue.

Bristol murmured an incoherent sound and dug her heels into the mattress. Her hips lifted restlessly. Her body writhed. Jesse didn't stop, didn't let up. When she began panting, he slid his palms up her body and rubbed the turgid points of her nipples between his thumb and forefingers.

When her body tightened and her skin flushed, he knew she rushed toward climax. Her heavy breathing turned to keening wails.

"And you're mine." He slid up her body, his thumb still working her clit as it hardened to stone. "Aren't you?"

"Yes."

"Say my name," he demanded. "I want to hear you scream it as you come."

"Jesse." Her voice broke as she strained toward the pleasure.

It was one of the most beautiful sights he'd ever seen.

But he wanted to be with Bristol, inside her and a part of her, share ecstasy with her. The two of them together. Now. Always.

The melody he'd been writing for her turned louder in his head. As he reached for a condom and rolled it on, lyrics began pelting his brain. Words they'd spoken to one another. Words they hadn't yet exchanged but he hoped like hell they would. Words of reverence. Promises. Vows.

She cried out in protest because he'd lifted his hand from her moments before bliss crashed over her, but he had something better. Thank goodness she was close because seeing her unabashed, honest pleasure was undoing him fast as fuck.

"Take me," he growled, sliding between her taut thighs.

Bristol eased them open as he shoved them wide. In seconds, he'd aligned his cock with her slick channel and tunneled in.

Sensation rained down on him. Bristol felt hot and tight, yeah. But so much more. Receptive and giving. Alive. Perfect. She was everything to Jesse, and he couldn't believe that he'd found her mere days ago. In the first hour, he'd known that she was different. By the end of the first night, he'd suspected she was truly special. Now he felt an urge all the way to his soul to make her his.

Gripping her thighs, he plunged in to the hilt. A sizzle shuddered down her spine. He plastered his hands flat on the bed and tried to make his way deeper, crawl all the way inside her. He rocked against Bristol as she whimpered in his ear.

"Jesse…" Her high-pitched voice sounded desperate, and that did all kinds of things to him.

He lowered himself to his elbows and slanted his lips over hers, slipping inside her mouth as he thrust deeper. He synched up both motions, making love to her mouth as he did her body. And god, she made love back to him, clutching at his shoulders, her thighs clinging to his hips, her female flesh gripping him so tightly that every move he made incited friction that ignited pleasure.

The music spun in his head, their rapid breaths and hearts mingling in a thumping backbeat that drove him up higher. The taste of her sweetness spilled onto his tongue. The rest of her body fit against him as if she'd been molded to be his. Somewhere in the back of his head, Jesse realized he was being more fucking poetic about a female than he ever been in his life.

But he finally understood why people had been writing songs about love for millennia. It wasn't just a jolt that rattled him. It was a mammoth force tearing through his every preconceived notion about the meaning of life, about devotion. The feeling was dense and enormous. It sat on his chest like a weight. Yet the thought of sharing his tomorrows with her freed him. He could breathe when he was lost inside her. In fact, Jesse began to wonder if he could ever really breathe again without her.

Her nails dug into his back now. She broke their kiss and looked up at him with worry and wonder and tears as he sank into her again and again. Damn if he didn't feel answering tears in his eyes. Damn if this didn't feel like forever.

Bliss overtook her face as her mouth gaped open. She clenched around his shuttling cock. Her body tensed. Her lids fluttered shut and she raced toward the pinnacle.

Jesse wanted to fall over the edge with her.

He ramped up his pace. "Say my name."

"Yes. Yes! *Jesse!*" she cried to the rafters.

Bristol bucked underneath him, her sex pulsing and clutching, clinging as he rode her through the mewling orgasm. But his own desire roared to the fore, smashing his defenses like a freight train. As the climax hit, it shocked then flattened him. He felt crushed. Yet he soared. And he clutched her as if he'd never let go again. With the sound of her cry ringing in his ears and the music he'd been crafting for her lilting in his head, he groaned long and low as he released, relinquishing way more than his desire.

He gave her his heart.

As the last wave of pleasure settled, Jesse caught his breath and looked into her eyes. He had no doubt that she was the thing that had been missing from his life. She was the one who would hold his hands for the rest of their days.

He dragged in a ragged breath. "Bristol Alexa Reece, I love you."

"Really?" She bit her lip, her lashes fluttering against her rosy cheeks.

"Yeah. This isn't merely some post-orgasm glow. I know the difference. I enjoy being with you. I'd rather be with you than everyone else." He shook his head. "Hell, I'm writing a song for you, about you. I haven't done that in years. You amaze me. You inspire me."

Bristol's face tightened. Her mouth turned down. Tears flowed. "I love you, too." Then she laughed. "God, we sound crazy."

"I'm about to sound crazier." He swallowed. "Marry me."

Chapter Seven

"He proposed!" Bristol squealed as she rushed downstairs to relieve Jayla of her temporary duty, anxious to bend her bestie's ear.

"Hayden? Because if he did, I'm gonna kill that jerk." Jayla finished putting some cash in the register, then turned to look at her. "Never mind. Hayden didn't do *that* to you." She grinned. "He couldn't do that. Jamie did, I'll bet. Girl, you look more like he propositioned you. And you accepted—thoroughly."

Bristol flushed. "That's not important."

"Orgasms are always important."

She looked around the restaurant to make sure no one else was nearby. "Jamie isn't Jamie. He's... You should sit down." She dragged a gaping Jayla to the nearest table and all but shoved her in a chair.

"What the hell? Who is he?"

"Jesse McCall."

Jayla looked blank for a second, then she scowled as if Bristol had lost her mind. "You're sure."

"Completely. When I figured it out, he fessed up."

"You're saying the world-famous singer bailed you out at Bubba Oink's Bone Yard and pretended to be your boyfriend, then went home with you and rocked your world before he *proposed?*"

When Jayla said it like that, the notion sounded absolutely crazy. Some of Bristol's excitement deflated.

"Yes."

"After knowing you for only a few days? And you mean he proposed marriage, right? Not some crazy three-way like he used to have."

"Marriage." She winced. "Yes."

"And what did you say?" Jayla leveled her with an insistent stare.

"I haven't answered him yet." She bit her lip. "It sounds ridiculous. Romantic, even. But I want to say yes."

"But you didn't. Something stopped you. There's a reason."

"I don't know. On the one hand, it feels sudden. But...when I'm with Jesse, I'm so happy. He's not the guy we see in the press. He's changed."

Jayla shot her a skeptical scowl. "They all say that. Why does he want to marry you?"

"He says he loves me. I-I think I love him, too. I realize we haven't known one another long and I still need to learn tons about him but...he's a better man than Hayden. In some ways, he even reminds me of Daddy."

Her best friend took her hand. "What would you do about this place?"

That had been one of her hesitations. "I don't know."

"Would you go on the road with him, like another one of his groupies?"

Now Jayla's voice sounded soft. It held notes of pity that made Bristol cringe. "I don't know. I guess we could figure it out. He says he's sober and wants to change his life—and he wants me at the center."

"Or more likely he wants to change his image. Girl..." Jayla squeezed her fingers. "An international star says he loves you and wants to marry you after a few days and you're not suspicious? C'mon, now... He's in a tough spot. His album is doing well but he's getting skewered in the press. The late-night hosts have made him into a punch line. What better way to convince people that he's changed than to tie the knot with a pretty little country girl who bakes sweets for a living? If he did, the whole narration about his character would change overnight. Right now, the story is party monger and manwhore sinks to a new low. But if he married you, suddenly they'd talk about how, after learning some hard lessons, he'd discovered an uplifting love in the face of tragedy. He'd be a role model." She snorted. "A freaking hero."

Everything Jayla said was true—and Bristol didn't want to hear it. "He wouldn't do that."

But did she know him well enough to say that for sure? How far would a man with a career as big as his go to save it?

"I'm not pointing this out to hurt you. I'm only saying it because I love you. Hayden mostly hurt your pride, but I think you've really fallen for Jesse. He could tear out your heart. Be really careful."

The message Bristol heard was that she couldn't possibly be interesting enough to keep a man like McCall, who jet-setted around the world and slept with beautiful people. She bit her lip, fearing Jayla was right. Everything had seemed so clear and real and natural when she'd been with Jesse, discussing their future. He adored her lack of worldly ways.

But was that true for his heart or merely his image?

"I don't know what to do," she murmured. "He wants to get married right away."

"Did he mention a prenuptial agreement?"

She frowned. "Actually, I'm the one who brought it up. People like him don't get married without one. And I just thought..."

"People like him? If he's going to be your husband, he's supposed to be your equal." Jayla's expression softened as she shook her head. "Think about this. Rushing you to the altar only benefits him. But you're putting yourself in an awkward position if you marry him without thinking this through. If he's not one hundred percent serious about being in love with you and he can't follow through as a real husband, you'll get dragged through the press. There are only two ways that goes: Either you're the naive little girl he grew bored with and everyone will pity you. Or you're the whore who broke his heart because you didn't stay by his side when your hoo-ha could have healed his emotional boo-boos. Either way, your life will never be the same."

Bristol sighed, her shoulders slumping. "Why are you always right? You were right about Hayden, too."

Jayla shrugged, her hair in black waves that dipped behind her shoulders. "Because I'm not in the middle of your situation, I can be more detached. Don't forget how much of an ass I made out of myself about D'Shaun last year."

Despite the concern swimming in her head, Bristol gave her friend a wry smile. "That was epic."

"So unless you're trying to one-up me, I think you should proceed with a whole lot of caution."

Suddenly, every muscle in Bristol's body ached as she stood. "Do you mind closing up for me?"

"What are friends for?" Jayla hugged her. "Think carefully. Do what's right for you."

Yeah. Now Bristol had to figure out what that was.

* * * *

Jesse emerged from the bedroom and donned his pants, searching the cozy apartment for his phone. He had to record all the new stuff about the song that had rushed through his head while he'd been making love to Bristol. And he supposed he should tell Candia that he might be getting married. Maybe.

Hell, he wished he knew how to convince Bristol that the amount of time they'd known one another didn't matter and that all the details would work themselves out. He'd help her find a way to either keep her bakery open here or open another elsewhere—or do whatever she wanted. All he cared about was making sure she was happy...by his side, as his wife.

But he understood her hesitation, her need to think things through. He just didn't like it.

During his search, he spotted the cinnamon rolls she'd left him earlier wrapped in foil. They were still a bit warm, and the icing dripping off them had his mouth watering. If he didn't love this woman for what was in her heart, he'd probably love her for her baking talent alone.

The first bite made him moan, and he leaned against the counter, head back, eyes closed. All this goodness from Bristol, both her words and her pastries, was good for his soul.

When he opened them again, he spotted his phone across the room on the coffee table. Dashing over to the device, he punched in the security code. His texts popped up. Candia had left him a message about two hours ago.

Morning! I've been researching your new girlfriend. Cute. Clean. The press will like her. I had a powwow with some of my peers. We all think she's good for your image. Announce that she's your new girlfriend. Or better yet, your fiancée. That will go miles to taking the attention off the crap about Ryan and the Harris girl. If you're up for it, a real wedding would totally improve the public's perception of you. I know it's quick but think about it...

Jesse sucked in a breath. Was she kidding? Ask someone to marry him for show?

Hell no! He wanted Bristol to marry him because he loved her and they would be good together. She would fill his heart, and he would fill her life.

With an impatient growl, he punched up Candia's contact and hit the call button. After three rings, the call went to voicemail. "Are you crazy, woman? I'm not going to pretend to marry Bristol for my image. I know your job is to worry what people think of me, but that's fucking out of the question. And over the line. I'm finally in love and I'm grabbing her with both hands. You can either be happy for me and get on board or hop the fuck off the train."

Jesse hung up and realized that Candia probably thought he'd gone crazy or been whipped by some magical unicorn pussy. But when she met Bristol, his publicist would love her, too. Yes, Candia knew exactly how to spin this to his advantage. She was like a killer shark scenting chum sometimes, and he didn't expect to curb her instinct, but he wasn't going to deceive Bristol to make his life easier.

Shoving the thought aside, he dashed to the sofa and quickly recorded the song that had been dancing in his head since making love to Bristol. He could hear the soft build of a steel guitar, something he never used. But it lent the song a heartfelt, somewhat country feel that reminded him of Bristol. The romantic strains of a piano accompanied as the bridge built to the chorus. He hummed where he didn't yet have lyrics, but the whole melody flowed naturally. It was beautiful and perfect for him.

Just like Bristol.

Yeah, he definitely sounded like he'd been whipped by some magical unicorn pussy. But he'd finally felt a real connection to a woman that didn't begin and end with his penis. Seeing her smile made him feel warm inside. Hearing her laugh thrilled him. So fucking sue him if he was feeling all Hallmark. He was happy. After over a decade of misery, he couldn't wait for the next ten years.

When he closed the app, he glanced at the clock. Shit, Bristol would be closing her bistro and coming upstairs soon. Since she'd never gotten to the hospital with those goodies yesterday, he thought they could run them up today—and start planning a wedding. She hadn't said yes yet, but he'd do or say whatever until she did.

Shakespurr chose that moment to jump on him and dig his dainty paws onto Jesse's lap, as if looking for a comfortable place to nap. He set the phone aside and picked up the feline. He'd never been much of a cat person, but Shakespurr met his gaze with an inquisitive stare before his lids turned heavy. Jesse stroked the cat, who immediately lived up to his name by letting loose a loud, dramatic purr.

With a laugh, he carried the cat into the bathroom, then eased him onto a rug and started the shower. The feline darted off at the sudden gush of the running water.

"Not a fan of baths, huh?" He chuckled and doffed his jeans, diving under the warm spray.

As he washed up, he hummed a few bars of Bristol's song, wondering if he could hire someone like David Tutera to pull off a huge wedding by the fall. Then again, that may not be what Bristol wanted. And the thought of speaking vows over helicopters hovering to get a shot of the ceremony wasn't his idea of romantic. Maybe a destination wedding in the Caribbean or Europe. No, she'd want her family near her. As crappy as they could be, Bristol was a girl who valued family, and she wouldn't get married without them. He made a mental note to ask Jayla about a pretty barn or church nearby and see if Bristol wanted to pledge her life to his there.

As he rinsed the last of his shampoo, he heard what sounded like his phone ringing. Candia most likely. Besides being dripping wet, Jesse didn't want to tangle with a Latina woman who had a temper to match after he'd left her that scathing message. He'd call back when she calmed down. But on the third ring, it stopped. With a shrug, he soaped up and rinsed off, then stepped out of the shower and wrapped a towel around his waist.

When he peeked out the bathroom door, he saw Bristol sitting on the sofa, holding Shakespurr to her chest and crooning to him.

"Hey, honey. Jayla closing up for you?"

She paused. Froze, really. He frowned, watching as she petted the cat one more time and set him on the cushion beside her. She didn't meet his gaze. "Yeah. But she had some questions for me. They're valid, and I think we should talk about them."

Jesse didn't like the sound of that but he'd do whatever it took to ease her fears. "Sure. What do you want to ask?"

"This marriage is really sudden. Why me?"

"Because I love you." Jesse crossed the room and picked up the feline, setting him on the back of the plushy couch so he could sit beside her.

"After only a few days?" She sounded skeptical.

He wanted to give Jayla a piece of his mind for planting doubt in Bristol's head, but if any of his friends had ever said they wanted to get married after a few days of "dating," he would have thought they were insane, too. "It may not sound logical, but it's love. It's not predictable. Sometimes when you know, you just know. I've spent way too many years being cynical. It's great to finally listen to my heart."

"What's the hurry to get married?"

Her guarded expression whacked him like a pain in the chest. "What's the point of waiting? I love you. You love me. If you want to plan a big event, we can. Or hell, let's elope. I don't care if we say our vows bungee jumping. But when you've lived with the superficial as long as I have and something real comes along, it smacks you in the face. I don't want to wait any longer to spend our lives together."

"And you're not asking me to marry you for a simple fix to your image?"

Dread detonated in the bottom of his stomach and spread outward. How was he supposed to erase this doubt when marriage would so obviously help him? "What did Candia say to you?"

"What does that mean?"

Her face had no expression, as if she was determined to keep it unreadable. There was definitely something going on in her head.

Jesse scowled. "Somehow, she's made you think that you're nothing to me but a quick fix for my PR problem. And it's total, utter bullshit."

"I don't think so." Tears trembled in her eyes as she held up his phone. "I read the text she sent you."

Oh, shit. "Bristol—"

"Not a word, you snake. You can't deny this." She sniffled. "When I came in to talk, your phone was ringing. I didn't think and I grabbed it to answer, but I was too late. Before I put it down, her text appeared. She told you to propose because I would be perfect for your image rehab."

"You've got this wrong."

"I don't think so." She stood, fists balls, face flushing with anger. "You lied to me. You used me. All your pretty words…"

"That's not how it happened. I'd already proposed when she sent that message."

"No. She sent it hours before your little impassioned speech."

"I was asleep when she sent that message," he pointed out.

She scoffed. "Or you pretended to be."

"Seriously?" He stood and stared down at her, water dripping from his hair. He swiped it away with an impatient hand. "You think I would flat-out lie to you after I know what you've been through? After I've poured out my heart to you?"

"I think you have a career to preserve and millions of fans to make happy. Who cares about my feelings when all that is at stake?"

"I do. If I didn't, why would I have jumped in to help you save face in front of your family the night we met? Why would I have chased Hayden off? Why would I do my best to tell you how special you are? Why would I have bothered to get to know you or tell you I love you? If all I wanted was to improve my fucking image, I could have paid someone a hundred times over to pretend to be my fiancée."

She had to see that logic. He'd been in far worse PR scrapes—the time with the three hookers in Rio came to mind—and hadn't resorted to a fake wedding. Didn't Bristol get that if he wanted a facade, he could find one anywhere?

"I don't know." She jumped up and paced. "I don't understand anything. It's all happening too fast and the timing is a bit too coincidental. I can't..." Bristol shook her head, plopping his phone onto the glass table. It pinged and rattled as she headed for the door. "I need to think."

"Where are you going?" he demanded.

"Away." She sobbed and sniffled.

"You're leaving?" he marched after her. "Don't do this. Honey, I meant every word I said. I really do love you."

She wrenched the door open and paused outside the threshold, then turned back to him with tears in her eyes. "I love you, too. And that's what hurts the most. I don't know if you're the love of my life...or my biggest mistake."

Before he could say a word, she slammed the door behind her. He would have given chase, but he wore only a towel. By the time he dressed, she'd be long gone. Already, he heard her footsteps pounding down the stairs, then across the wooden subfloor of the stock room. A door slammed. He looked out the window, watching her flee to her car and drive away.

"Well, fuck." He pounded a fist into the door, then grabbed his phone and reread Candia's text. Yeah, that would look bad out of context. Damn it.

Jesse sighed. He wanted to be pissed but he understood her reservations. Trust was hard for her after Hayden had screwed her over so thoroughly. Jesse knew she had no way of knowing the man he'd been without her, and he wasn't sure how to prove that he couldn't be more serious about their marriage. But he had to start thinking fast because he didn't intend to lose her.

Chapter Eight

With a sinking dread, Bristol parked down the street from her mother's yellow Victorian and crawled out of her crappy compact. Tuesday evening dinner, and clearly she was one of the last to arrive since everyone else's cars lined the crumbling tar road on both sides.

She closed the door and leaned against the vehicle, head bowed, and let out a rough breath. Might as well end this circus. The sooner she told everyone that "Jamie" had ditched her, the sooner she could start living with the label of Lewisville's sad sack ho-bag/spinster and get back to her small apartment where she'd see Jesse everywhere and wonder again if she'd been stupid to run him off.

From the direction of her mother's house, Jayla came sprinting across the wide, open yard. "Have you heard from him?"

Bristol had no doubt which "him" her bestie was referring to. "No. Nothing."

After their argument, she'd left, taking a ride over to the Sonic Drive-In east of Lewisville, in the town of Stamps. A milkshake and a good cry later, she'd headed back to her apartment, ready to work things through. Jesse—and every trace of him—had been gone.

Only then did she realize that she didn't have his number. And it wasn't as if she could simply hit up his website or Facebook page and leave a comment that read, *Hey, Jesse proposed to me. Could you tell him I want to talk so he should call me?*

Jayla curled an arm around her. "I know you thought you loved him but…maybe him leaving so abruptly was his way of admitting that the jig is up."

"Yeah." Admitting that possibility seemed to take all of her breath. After that, she didn't have any air for the rest of her body. Her shoulders slumped. She felt half dead inside. Last night, she'd had to change the sheets before she could sleep because they smelled like him.

And his absence had torn her in two.

"It'll get better," her friend promised.

"It's just…he defended himself so vehemently. He swore that he loved me and wanted to get married. He said I was trying to make matters of the heart logical, and when I was drowning in my banana cream pie milkshake, I kind of wondered if he was right. I still do."

"Hang in there." Jayla hugged her, and Bristol reveled in her friend's embrace for a silent moment. The woman might not be her biological sibling, but she was the sister of her heart. Bristol felt blessed every day to have her.

"I'll try. Thanks."

"I'm glad you're here. I might have mentioned to Presleigh that Hayden came to see you after church on Sunday. Apparently, he told her he was going home to take a 'nap.'" Jayla held up air quotes.

"He only stayed a few minutes, and nothing happened, except that he behaved like an ass."

"That's nothing new," Jayla drawled.

"Nope. Besides, he'd been to see Corey before me." Or that's what he'd said. "He probably spent most of his time there."

"What?" Jayla pulled a disapproving face. "Corey left on Sunday morning to go meet that girl he met on the Internet, the one who lives in Arkadelphia."

"Oh, that's right. I forgot. Maybe Hayden did, too." She shrugged.

"Or he remembered that Corey's lonely little sister quit University of Arkansas and moved back home."

Bristol wanted to say that Hayden wouldn't cheat on Presleigh…but she knew firsthand that he totally would.

"Whatever happened on Sunday, Presleigh is having one hell of a righteous snit right now. Hayden is trying to suck up but…"

"He's terrible at it."

"You know that's right." Jayla shook her head.

Bristol had to grin. She could just picture five-foot-two, eyes-of-blue Presleigh's tizzy. Then she tried to imagine self-absorbed Hayden struggling to grasp why his fiancée might be upset. She rolled her eyes.

"Well, that's something to look forward to." Because Bristol certainly wasn't eager for the rest of dinner and having to explain to everyone that her "boyfriend" had left. "Let's get this over with."

Jayla turned and started leading her toward the party. "I saw on one of the entertainment websites today that Jesse attended his bandmate's funeral this morning. He spoke. It was really touching."

Yeah, she'd look that right up on YouTube. Not. Well, all right...she probably would. "I'm glad he went. I think he needed that closure."

And maybe that would enable him to start the rest of his life with a clean slate so he could find a way to be happy. Bristol wanted that for him more than anything.

As she and Jayla crossed the yard together and opened her mother's bright-white front door, the wreath of silk daisies nearly bapped her in the face and stirred up a little cloud of dust. But as soon as she heard the shouting from inside, the sneeze burning in her nose dissipated.

"I'm going to kill you," a man growled on the far side of the foyer wall, seemingly from inside the kitchen.

Bristol didn't recognize that voice. She whirled on Jayla, her gaze asking if she knew who was making the threat.

Her friend shrugged.

"Wait a minute." She recognized that insistent voice. Hayden's pal, Corey.

Jayla absently smacked the front door shut, then grabbed her arm to haul her toward the action so they didn't miss anything.

"Was this going on when you came out to get me?" Bristol whispered.

"No, girl. If it had been, you would have been on your own. You know how to find the door." Jayla grinned.

Together, they rounded the corner to find a crowd gathered and Hayden up in Corey's face, his shirt in her ex-boyfriend's fists. "How the hell could you do this to me?"

Do what? Bristol couldn't tell by looking at the two of them.

Then Presleigh ran across the room, tear-splattered mascara running down her face. "Bris... Help me."

Automatically, she opened her arms to her younger sister, who crashed into her and began sobbing anew. Presleigh held her tightly, all but cutting off Bristol's breath. Absently, she stroked her sibling's blonde curls and slanted Jayla a confused glance.

"Now, boys..." Her mother tried to step in. "Let's talk this out."

Hayden snarled at Linda Mae. "Butt out."

Her mother jumped back with a startled gasp and a hand over her mouth.

Corey looked around the crowded kitchen as if frantic for a lifeline. No one came to his rescue.

"What's the matter?" Bristol murmured to her sister.

Presleigh stared up at her with big blue eyes, swimming in angst. "I'm pregnant."

Hadn't Hayden said two days ago that she was a virgin waiting for her wedding night? Bristol frowned.

"Why is Hayden mad at Corey? Did he tell everyone about the baby before you were ready?"

"No." She gulped then hiccupped. "Corey is the father."

When Presleigh dropped her gaze in shame, shock slid through Bristol. She snapped her stare around to Jayla, who looked equally stunned.

"When did you find out?" she murmured to her sister.

"This morning. Hayden came over to talk to me. I..." She shook her head. "I wasn't thinking. I left the home pregnancy test in the trash can. And he saw it."

Holy cow! Talk about the unexpected... Bristol's head reeled.

"When did this thing with Corey start?"

"When Hayden started screwing my sister about three months ago," Corey cut in, jerking away from Hayden's raised fist with a glower of his own. "Sarah came crying to me one night that Hayden wouldn't break it off with Presleigh even though he hooked up with her almost every day. I knew talking to Hayden wouldn't do me any good, so I called Presleigh."

"I didn't believe it at first, but when he started going over to Corey's house a lot when Corey wasn't there, I knew. Besides, Sarah always shot me mean glances and had hickies on her neck."

Bristol grabbed her sister by the shoulders and held her at arm's length. "Why didn't you call off the wedding?"

"At first, I hoped I could turn it around. Then...I kind of fell for Corey. But the invitations were already out and the dress was ordered...and I was confused."

"All this time you kept telling me that you were waiting so your first time could be on our wedding night, you were sneaking around behind my back and giving it up to my best friend."

"Don't go there, asshole!" Presleigh charged toward him.

Bristol held her sister back. She'd rarely seen the girl raise her voice and never heard her swear, much less see her with a violent tendency.

Jayla reared back and did a double take, too.

"You started kissing on me while you were still dating my sister," Presleigh accused. "Everyone tried to tell me you're a manwhore, but I didn't want to listen. When I found out you were sleeping with Sarah, I got mad. Then I got drunk."

"And Corey helped you out by taking your virginity?" he asked snidely.

Her sister tore off her engagement ring and threw it at him. It bounced off his chest and pinged to the floor. "To hell with you! He's twice the man you'll ever be."

"How do you know? You never tried me." Hayden gave her a cocky smirk.

"Shut your mouth," Corey insisted, curling his hand into a beefy fist and punching Hayden in the nose. "You'll never deserve her."

Bristol resisted the urge to clap. Instead, she watched Hayden stumble back against the refrigerator door. Corey ran toward Presleigh, arms outstretched. He kissed her, grabbing onto her as if she was the most precious thing in the world to him. She melted against him as if he was her knight in shining armor.

What the hell?

With a sharp elbow, Jayla jabbed Bristol in the ribs. "You had no idea?"

"None." She'd kind of been avoiding them both after their betrayal. She'd have to learn to forgive her sister someday. Hayden… She smiled. Looked like he was history.

Linda Mae stepped forward again and picked up Presleigh's engagement ring from the floor. "I think you should be going."

He took one look at Presleigh and Corey, still sucking face in the middle of the commotion, then gritted his teeth. "Gladly."

On his way out, he bumped Bristol's shoulder as if he wanted to punish her, too. She'd had more than enough of him and grabbed the annoying jerk by the collar. "I'm sorry. You were going to say that, right? I know an apology must have been on the tip of your tongue. Because you certainly couldn't be so rude as to bump me on purpose when you're the cheating bastard who left me for my own sister, then ditched her for an easy lay. Tell me you aren't that big of a rat bastard."

Hayden stared as if poised to say something but then reconsidered. "Bristol, what's gotten into you?"

"A whole lot of anger. Thanks to you, I was stupid enough to let myself lose—"

The doorbell cut her off, and Bristol fumed that she didn't get a chance to lay into Hayden about how he'd done a number on her ability to trust and most likely contributed to the reason she no longer had Jesse beside her.

But Hayden decided he'd been saved by the bell and darted away when she loosened her grip to peer around the kitchen wall, back into the foyer. He sprinted out as if someone had set his ass on fire.

Standing next to her, Jayla laughed. Corey and Presleigh came up for air.

Linda Mae looked on. "It's not too late for that June wedding. We'll simply have another groom."

Bristol tried not to roll her eyes. Since it seemed as if no one else was interested in answering the door, she used it to make her escape, striding around the corner to find Hayden hustling down the walk and a very polished brunette in a gray business suit standing at the portal.

Her heart stuttered. Bristol hesitated, staring at the stranger. "Can I help you?"

Please let her have some connection to Jesse.

"Hi." She stuck out her hand. "I'm Candia."

Bristol blew out a jagged breath. She wasn't shocked…but she wasn't thrilled, either. "Don't tell me you're here to plead his case about any sort of fake marriage. The answer is no."

"I'm here to apologize," she clarified, hands clasped, face contrite. "May I come in so I can explain?"

What the hell? The night had already turned into a freaking sideshow. "Sure."

Candia stepped in, and Bristol shut the door behind her, looking around for some privacy. Obviously, they couldn't talk in the kitchen with everyone listening in. So she guided the woman into the empty parlor off the foyer to the right and shut the door. Instantly, the noise level dropped.

"Why are you here?" The more Bristol thought about it, the more she wished she'd shut the door in the woman's face. "You know, I'm a real person with feelings who doesn't appreciate you trying to manipulate me in order to make your client's life a little cushier. He can go to—"

"Before you finish that sentence, you should know that marrying you was his idea first."

Knowing that Jesse McCall thought it was no big deal to twist her heart around and pretend to be enough in love with her to share a lifelong bond pissed her off. "Great. Thanks for the FYI. You're both horrible human beings. Will you get out of my house, please?"

Well, her mother's house, but she was splitting hairs. The worst part was, even as Candia was throwing Jesse under the bus and all but admitted they'd conspired to use her to improve his image, Bristol still wanted him, missed him. Kind of even loved him.

Exactly why she hated romance. She did it so spectacularly bad and always wound up hurt. From now on, she was banning both romance *and* flings. Instead, she'd become the crazy cat spinster who baked cookies for the whole damn town. Maybe it wouldn't bother her in a few years.

Yeah, when you're sixty.

As she reached around Candia to open the door and show the woman out, Jesse's publicist shook her head. "That's not what I meant. The idea to marry you because he loves you was his. I had the same idea, though for the more obvious reason I stated in my message. I texted him…which I hear you read. When he read it first, this is what he had to say." She held up her phone to reveal the screen that listed her voicemails. One from Jesse appeared three messages down, the date and time stamp shortly after he had made love to her and proposed.

"Are you crazy, woman?" Jesse sounded really agitated. No, super pissed off. "I'm not going to pretend to marry Bristol for my image. I know your job is to worry what people think of me, but that's fucking out of the question. And over the line. I'm finally in love and I'm grabbing her with both hands. You can either be happy for me and get on board or hop the fuck off the train."

Candia stopped the voicemail, then flipped to her texts. "You can see clearly here what time he read my message." She shoved the screen in Bristol's face. Based on what she remembered, Jesse hadn't read Candia's text until after he'd asked Bristol to marry him.

Her heart seized up. Regret poured through her. Had Jesse actually meant everything he said?

Had she completely screwed up?

She jerked her stare up to Candia's face, her heart racing. The sort of cold sweat that came with a terrible realization hit her. "You're not here to try and convince me to marry him for his image?"

She shook her head, looking contrite. Given Candia's polished-within-an-inch-of-her-life appearance, Bristol was pretty sure she didn't show anyone her vulnerable underbelly very often.

"I'm here because Jesse is not merely a client; he's a friend. He was also right. What I suggested was over the line. I didn't understand how you could have possibly made such an impact on him in such a short period of time, but since he circled back with me last night, he's set up a scholarship for recovering addicts in Maddy Harris's name. At about one this morning, he filmed a PSA about the dangers of recreational drug use and experimenting. I can't tell you how many favors he called in for that. Then he sat me down and told me everything wonderful about you. In the four years I've known him, he's never connected with any woman on anything beyond the physical level. But you, he can't stop talking about. To hear him, you're practically a saint. Since you agreed to be your sister's maid of honor after she stole your ex, I'd say that qualifies." The woman sent her a wry grin.

"They just broke up. I'm off the hook." Bristol blinked at the other woman, confused. "I'm sorry. So…you came here to tell me what a great guy he is and how much I screwed up?"

"No. He wanted me to be sure you understood that what I said in that text wasn't his idea, but mine. All mine. And he wants to talk to you."

Bristol bit her lip as her heart skidded to a stop. Jesse didn't hate her for lacking trust and assuming he was screwing her over? For once, she didn't hesitate. She knew exactly what she wanted. "Yes. I want to talk to him, too. I wanted to talk to him after inhaling my milkshake."

When Candia looked at her blankly, Bristol tried not to curse at herself. The conversation had rattled her. She needed to be clear before the woman decided she was crazy and tried to change Jesse's mind for good.

"Sorry." She grimaced. "That didn't make sense."

Candia suddenly grinned. "No, I get it now. After a breakup, men cry in their beers. Women consume empty calories and have a good cry."

The woman's words gave Bristol pause. "He didn't break his sobriety, did he?"

"No. In the past, I think an emotional loss like that would have sent him to a bottle and some blow with a couple of bimbos. Last night, he was completely determined to get you back."

Her words made Bristol's heart swell and beat faster. The misery that had dragged her down since she'd returned from Sonic to find him gone had magically disappeared. In its place? Hope.

"So will he call me or something?"

"Something," she replied vaguely, then held out her hand. "It was really nice to meet you."

Bristol shook it, then Jesse's publicist exited the parlor and whisked her way out the front door. She stood, gaping after the woman. That was it?

Suddenly, Jayla appeared at her side. "Who was that?"

With a frown, Bristol started to explain. Granted, in slow, halting sentences because she was still trying to grasp it all herself. But the hope was shimmering brighter, like a shiny bangle dancing a jig in her brain.

Then the doorbell rang again, and she let out a sigh of relief. Maybe Candia had returned.

But when she wrenched the door open, Bristol found Jesse McCall standing there, looking far more like his rock star self than he had during his days with her. He wore combat boots and black leather pants—and he wore them well. A tight charcoal tee stretched across his muscled chest and hugged his bulging biceps. A fresh scruff now darkened his jawline, lending him a gorgeously disreputable look. A guitar strap crossed his torso diagonally, and the instrument rested on his back. The neck stood out, angled above one shoulder. He didn't look merely gorgeous, but as if the professional and personal side were finally happy together in his skin.

Bristol swallowed her tongue.

"Hi, honey. Sorry I'm late." He echoed the words he'd first spoken to her and sent her a searching smile, complete with those dimples that made her heart melt.

A thousand things she could say to him crossed her brain at once. A simple "hi" didn't begin to convey everything in her heart. But she didn't want to get into all the gory details of their relationship in the foyer of her mother's house while anyone could simply walk in. As it was, Bristol figured that only a miracle—or a major ongoing drama in the kitchen—was keeping everyone from running to the front door to see who'd arrived.

Jayla elbowed her, reminding Bristol that she hadn't said anything at all.

But her mouth didn't seem to be working. Instead, she launched herself at him, linking her hands behind his neck and plastering her body against his. "I'm sorry."

He banded a beefy hand around her waist and bowed his head until their foreheads touched. He stroked her crown with a soft palm. "It's all right. I understand. Hayden's crap, Jayla's questions, Candia's text..."

"They messed with my head," she agreed breathlessly.

"I sent Candia to explain since she had all the evidence on her phone. You better now?"

She nodded, then looked around to see that her best friend had melted into the background, probably in the kitchen doing crowd control. Bless her.

"Much." Bristol smiled brightly. "You're here."

"You ready to talk?"

"Yeah." But she wanted to make one thing clear first. "I love you."

"I love you, too. That song I was writing for you at your place? I finished it this morning. Can I play it for you? You'll be the very first person to hear it."

Her heart flipped and fluttered. "Please."

With the warmest smile she'd ever seen him give, he twisted the guitar strap around his body and anchored the instrument against his chest. He strummed and looked at her. He was all man, but she saw the uncertain boy under that who hoped she'd like his gift.

After he cleared his throat, he began singing in the beautiful tenor that had made him millions.

"You turned me on
Like a light bulb
With just a smile
And all your charm

You made me hot
My heart was frozen
All but closed down
Then you sparked me with a touch

And now you're gone
I'm so lost
Looking for a way to carry on

I can't go back
To who I was
To who I'd been
Don't want to hear 'God, remember him when…'

Before you
I didn't know what I wanted
Or know about love
I didn't understand
You're all I've dreamed of
But now you're gone
And I live with regret
I'm just not ready to handle it yet.

Before you
I didn't know you would change me
Or show me the way
I didn't understand
Why my pride wouldn't wait
But now I see
I understand
You've made me into a better man."

As he repeated the chorus, Bristol teared up. The drops rolled down her cheeks. He'd written those words about her? "It's beautiful. Oh, my gosh… I'm so honored. Touched." She choked. "In love with you. I wish I had something to give you in return."

"Right now, I only want one thing." He got down on one knee and drew out a pretty blue box from his pants.

She gasped. When she untied the white bow and pulled off the lid, a sleek black velvet box lay inside.

"Open it," he insisted softly.

She did so—and absolutely lost her breath. Inside was an exquisite Tiffany engagement ring. It wasn't beautiful because of its size or overwhelming dazzle, but because of its sparkling simplicity. It looked like something she would have picked out for herself.

She looked at him, fresh tears sparkling. "I love it."

"Marry me, Bristol Alexa Reese. We'll wait as long as you want to announce our engagement and tie the knot. We'll get married however you want and live wherever you want. I'm dissolving the band to go behind the scenes and focus on my songwriting. I swear no getting wasted or getting laid. I just want everything to be you and me and our lives forever."

Tears ran down her face quickly now. She sobbed at the feeling swelling in her chest, but she managed to choke out one word to him. "Yes."

A grin broke out across his handsome face. "No doubts?"

"None."

"What are you going to tell your family about me? About us."

"That I'm in love." She gave him a watery smile. "And to butt out."

He took the box from her shaking hands and settled the ring on her finger. "It's a perfect fit."

She raised up on her tiptoes and pressed a tender kiss to his lips, melting into him now and always. "Just like you are for me."

Sign up for the 1001 Dark Nights Newsletter
and be entered to win a Tiffany Key necklace.

There's a contest every month!

Go to www.1001DarkNights.com to subscribe.

As a bonus, all subscribers will receive a free
1001 Dark Nights story
The First Night
by Lexi Blake & M.J. Rose

Turn the page for a full list of the
1001 Dark Nights fabulous novellas...

1001 Dark Nights

WICKED WOLF by Carrie Ann Ryan
A Redwood Pack Novella

WHEN IRISH EYES ARE HAUNTING by Heather Graham
A Krewe of Hunters Novella

EASY WITH YOU by Kristen Proby
A With Me In Seattle Novella

MASTER OF FREEDOM by Cherise Sinclair
A Mountain Masters Novella

CARESS OF PLEASURE by Julie Kenner
A Dark Pleasures Novella

ADORED by Lexi Blake
A Masters and Mercenaries Novella

HADES by Larissa Ione
A Demonica Novella

RAVAGED by Elisabeth Naughton
An Eternal Guardians Novella

DREAM OF YOU by Jennifer L. Armentrout
A Wait For You Novella

STRIPPED DOWN by Lorelei James
A Blacktop Cowboys ® Novella

RAGE/KILLIAN by Alexandra Ivy/Laura Wright
Bayou Heat Novellas

DRAGON KING by Donna Grant
A Dark Kings Novella

PURE WICKED by Shayla Black
A Wicked Lovers Novella

HARD AS STEEL by Laura Kaye
A Hard Ink/Raven Riders Crossover

STROKE OF MIDNIGHT by Lara Adrian
A Midnight Breed Novella

ALL HALLOWS EVE by Heather Graham
A Krewe of Hunters Novella

KISS THE FLAME by Christopher Rice
A Desire Exchange Novella

DARING HER LOVE by Melissa Foster
A Bradens Novella

TEASED by Rebecca Zanetti
A Dark Protectors Novella

THE PROMISE OF SURRENDER by Liliana Hart
A MacKenzie Family Novella

FOREVER WICKED by Shayla Black
A Wicked Lovers Novella

CRIMSON TWILIGHT by Heather Graham
A Krewe of Hunters Novella

CAPTURED IN SURRENDER by Liliana Hart
A MacKenzie Family Novella

SILENT BITE: A SCANGUARDS WEDDING by Tina Folsom
A Scanguards Vampire Novella

About Shayla Black

Shayla Black is the *New York Times* and *USA Today* bestselling author of more than forty novels. For over fifteen years, she's written contemporary, erotic, paranormal, and historical romances via traditional, independent, foreign, and audio publishers. Her books have sold well over a million copies and been published in a dozen languages.

Raised an only child, Shayla occupied herself with lots of daydreaming, much to the chagrin of her teachers. In college, she found her love for reading and realized that she could have a career publishing the stories spinning in her imagination. Though she graduated with a degree in Marketing/Advertising and embarked on a stint in corporate America to pay the bills, her heart has always been with her characters. She's thrilled that she's been living her dream as a full-time author for the past seven years.

Shayla currently lives in North Texas with her wonderfully supportive husband, her teenage daughter, and a very spoiled cat. In her "free" time, she enjoys reality TV, reading, and listening to an eclectic blend of music.

Connect with me online:
Facebook: https://www.facebook.com/ShaylaBlackAuthor
Twitter: https://twitter.com/Shayla_Black
Website: www.ShaylaBlack.com
Instagram: https://instagram.com/ShaylaBlack/
YouTube: https://www.youtube.com/channel/UCFM7RZF38CqBlr6YG3a4mRQ

If you enjoyed this book, I would appreciate your help so others can enjoy it, too.

Recommend it. Please help other readers find this book by recommending it to friends, readers' groups and discussion boards.

Review it. Please tell other readers why you liked this book by reviewing it at Amazon or Goodreads. If you do write a review, please send me an e-mail at interact @ shaylablack.com so I can thank you with a personal e-mail.

Wicked for You
Wicked Lovers Book 10
By Shayla Black
Coming October 6, 2015

Ever since he rescued her from a dangerous kidnapper, Mystery Mullins has wanted Axel Dillon. When he returned her to her Hollywood father and tabloid life, she was grateful...and a little in love. Mystery wasn't ready to let Axel go, even after the soldier gently turned her away because, at nineteen, she was too young.

Now, six years later, Mystery is grown, with a flourishing career and a full life—but she's still stuck on Axel. Disguised, she propositions him in a bar, and the night they spend together is beyond her wildest dreams. Mystery steels herself to walk away—except the sheets are barely cold when her past comes back to haunt her.

Once he realizes Mystery isn't the stranger he thought, Axel is incensed and intrigued. But when it's clear she's in danger, he doesn't hesitate to become her protector—and her lover—again. And as the two uncover a secret someone is willing to kill for, Axel is determined to claim Mystery's heart before a murderer silences her for good.

* * * *

Axel Dillon . . . Even the thought of him turned her inside out.

Mystery glanced around the bar again, easing farther inside. Some biker types in the far corner playing pool eyed her. The bartender still stared down his pierced nose at her. Three cops huddled together all focused on her. Did they think she was casing the place for a robbery? She had to stop standing in the middle of the room like an idiot. *Take a seat and order a drink.*

Finally, her head forced her body to obey, and she eased into a little booth near the back. Once she'd seated herself, everyone around her started talking again. And from her new vantage point, she could see the back half of the bar, previously obscured by the wall of televisions.

There he sat, absently staring at ESPN and sipping a beer, his profile strong. As usual, his rugged face was unreadable. He still kept his dark-blond hair military short. And he still looked like the side of a mountain. Somewhere around six foot five, he'd always been built big, but in the last few years, she'd swear he'd put on another slab of muscle. His tight black T-shirt hugged every hard swell and lean dip, tapering past a flat belly to narrow hips. She had to hold in a sigh. Even a single glance of him made her heart knock against her ribs and everything below her waist tingle. Mystery swallowed.

He didn't once look her way. Somehow, she'd hoped their stares would lock. He would approach her, want her, and whisk her away for a spectacular night of unbridled sex that would blow away both her panties and her mind. That had been another one of her fantasies. Right now, he clearly had no idea she existed.

On shaky knees, she stood again and headed in his direction. She tried not to stare. A glance up at the television proved he watched a recap of a pro basketball game. With a grunt, he glanced down into the neck of his beer bottle as she slid onto the empty stool beside him.

Now that he was so near, Mystery could feel his body heat, smell him—rugged earth, cut wood, musk. Damn, being this close made her feel both safe and weak.

"Something on your mind?" He turned to her, his stare expectant.

She searched his expression and didn't see a hint of recognition on his large, blunt face. What a relief. But the cleft in his chin and his bright blue eyes still made her feel weak and wanting. That instant chemical attraction she'd felt years ago hadn't waned in the least.

"There is." She mimicked the British accents she'd been surrounded with since she'd fled the U.S.—and him—over six years ago.

Her assertion obviously surprised him. Though he narrowed his eyes, they pierced her.

"I'll bite. Lay it on me."

The bartender chose that moment to come around and plunk a napkin in front of her. "Now that you found a seat, you want a drink?"

A glass of vino sounded heavenly. "Do you have a wine list, please?"

He snorted. "No. I got three types: red, white, and pink."

Mystery paused. She hadn't expected anything private label, but surely more of a selection than that.

"Is the white a pinot grigio?"

The bartender looked as if he was losing patience. "I don't know what kind that is, but the jug of white I have is as close as I've got. You want some or not?"

That could be seriously terrible booze. She'd been willing to give up designer for the night and leave her Tiffany baubles at her hotel, but she'd spew if she drank the equivalent of Boone's Farm.

"Then I'll have a glass of water, please." Better to keep a clear head, anyway. "Thank you."

As he turned and grabbed a glass, the bartender shook his head and muttered something to himself. Mystery really didn't want to know what.

"I'm not sure what threw him off more, your accent or your request." The corner of Axel's mouth lifted in amusement, giving her a flash of dimples.

She'd forgotten the way his smile could soften his harsh face. She grinned back. "He seemed quite ruffled."

A moment later, the young, pierced guy set a glass in front of her with lots of ice and a bit of water, sans lemon. She blinked, and her colored contacts jabbed her eyes with a reminder of their existence. Or maybe it was a warning that her plan would likely fail spectacularly.

"So do you," Axel said. "I won't point out that I've never seen you here, but I'll guess you've never been to a place like this."

"Never," she admitted. "What gave me away?"

He chuffed. "Leaving the door open so you could gape with barely disguised horror was a start. I particularly liked the way you turned slightly green when you stared at the guys about to do to body shots with Trina." He nodded to the corner where the bearded men and the woman in the halter top all laughed. "So why are you here?"

She'd forgotten how observant he could be and how accurately he could draw conclusions. He did it in an instant, as if nothing in the world shocked him anymore. The world still shocked her all the time.

She hadn't, however, forgotten how direct he was.

"Curious," she lied and held in a wince at her lame answer.

He shrugged. "Let me try another way: The place is more than half empty, so why did you sit next to me?"

Brutally direct, she mentally corrected.

Mystery gaped for an answer. "Why not?"

In retrospect, she could have been a little less obvious and a little more coy in choosing a seat. Maybe she should have sat a few stools away, ordered some terrible wine, and seen if he'd struck up a conversation. But she'd taken one look at him, and any thought of careful or logical had flown out the window.

He leveled her with a disbelieving stare. "That's all you've got? You couldn't even have come up with a good lie?"

Not really. She could have gone the "You look familiar" route, but that would have been too close to the truth. As far as she could see, that only left her one tactic.

"You're very attractive. Pardon me for being interested."

A little smile lit up his eyes before he took another swig of beer. "I didn't say you being close upset me. You're attractive yourself." He stared a moment longer, then glanced down at his empty beer before he shifted his attention to her untouched glass. "You sure I can't get you something stronger to drink? I can't believe a girl like you would risk life and limb to come to this dive for a swig of water."

Truth was, drinking didn't hold a lot of appeal for her. In the past, she pretended otherwise, but . . . "While I appreciate the offer, I'm actually not interested in alcohol." She forced herself to meet his inquisitive stare. "Would you like to find somewhere more private to . . ."

"Talk?" He gave her an ironic curl of his lips.

"No." She sucked in a shaking breath. "To fuck. Would you be interested?"

On behalf of 1001 Dark Nights,
Liz Berry and M.J. Rose would like to thank ~

Steve Berry
Doug Scofield
Kim Guidroz
Jillian Stein
InkSlinger PR
Dan Slater
Asha Hossain
Chris Graham
Pamela Jamison
Jessica Johns
Dylan Stockton
Richard Blake
BookTrib After Dark
The Dinner Party Show
and Simon Lipskar

Made in the USA
San Bernardino, CA
08 September 2015